David Ayres

Top of the Sixties

Holland Park Press London

Published by Holland Park Press 2011

First Edition

A CIP catalogue record for this book is
available from The British Library.

ISBN 978-1-907320-09-5

Cover designed by Reactive Graphics

Printed and bound by CPI Group (UK) Ltd, Croydon, CR0 4YY

www.hollandparkpress.co.uk

The fourteen stories in *Top of the Sixties* celebrate a delightful world with the firm belief in progress, new youth culture and boundless optimism that define the 1960s.

David Ayres has a unique way of describing the lives of ordinary people, full of humour and empathy. His stories often contain an underlying hint of sensuality.

Through a colourful parade of characters we are shown what matters in life. Take, for example, fifteen-year-old Keith, who is working on Mr Davies' van, the grumpy yet good-hearted fruit and veg man, or Alastair, who is trying to find his feet in his first teaching job at a local comprehensive school. The quest for love, by the young and not so young, is masterfully woven into these tales by an experienced storyteller.

David Ayres has caught the mood of an era wonderfully, and although change is in the air, he also cleverly shows that certain things remain the same. The stories will generate a smile of recognition on the faces of readers who remember the 1960s. Yet readers of any age will recognise the universal emotions they convey, such as the painful self-consciousness only teenagers can feel or the appearance of love at any age. This collection really puts its finger on what makes people tick.

Each story can be read on its own, but together they paint a vivid picture of life in a small, tightly-knit working-class town in the Midlands during the 1960s.

A SACK OF SPUDS   9

THE LATIN GIRL   21

AWAKENING   35

THE DRAMA QUEEN   41

ALASTAIR'S TRIUMPH   49

ROMANY   63

BAZ TO THE SLAUGHTER   73

THE FARM STOP   85

SOMETHING FOR THE WEEKEND   91

WETTON MILL   101

FRET   111

OUT OF THE BOX   125

UNCLE JOE   143

A GIFT OF LILIES   157

The winter of 1961 was cold and snowy, although no one could have known how much worse the next one would be. There had been snow since early January. On the pavements dirty snow was piled up and the roads looked dark and slick. It felt as if it had been cold for ever, there had never been any summer. Darkness came earlier than usual, so that the snowy front lawns were lit orange by the street lamps.

At fourteen years of age Keith Golder looked ridiculous smoking a cigarette, yet he felt like a pop star with his upturned collar and Elvis Presley hair. He scooted his bicycle down the side entrance of the newly built semi into which his family had recently moved. He flicked his cigarette casually away, just as he'd seen them do in the movies, except that he fumbled it slightly and had to make an emergency stop to retrieve the glowing embers from his jeans turn-up. No swearing followed, because Keith was fully occupied shaking his burnt fingers in the icy darkness.

Leaving his bicycle in the little shed at the back, he yanked open the sticking back door to the kitchen and felt his young body relax as the warm fug enveloped him. He struggled out of his steaming coat and hung it on the pantry door handle. He was aware that his father had just pattered over the lino in his threadbare carpet slippers.

'Hi, Dad.' Keith struck a pose for no one in particular and gave a lopsided smile, rather like a sneer, which was very fashionable for the time.

'You're spending a lot of time with that Harding girl.' Keith's dad peered at him over his reading glasses, which consisted as much of Elastoplast as of any optical materials.

It crossed Keith's mind to say, 'What of it?', which would be suitably rebellious, but he knew better.

His father appraised him silently, then said, 'Your mother spoke to the fruit and veg man today.' Keith waited to hear how such an event could possibly concern him. His father raised his voice slightly, as if expecting resistance. 'His helper has moved house and Mr Davies is looking for another young lad to help out on his fruit and veg round.'

Keith's heart sank and a host of objections swam into his mind, not least the freezing cold involved in working on a van which was open at the back. His father went on, raising his right hand to ward off any argument, though Keith thought he looked like a retired traffic policeman, standing like that against the kitchen sink.

'You've got to help out in this house, lad. Your paper round finished ages ago. You can't just sit around here playing your Roy Shannon records and cavorting with the Harding girl.'

'No, Dad, it's Roy Orbison and Del Shannon, not Roy...'

'All right, all right, I don't care who they are, long-haired louts, the lot of them. You get ready to pull your socks up and help me and your mother out. Your sister baby-sits. She does her bit. It's time you did yours.'

The Dansette de Luxe threatened to shake the cluttered little lounge to pieces, as Del Shannon's 'Runaway' was delivered at full volume. The door flew open and bounced off the arm of the settee.

'For God's sake, Keith! Turn it down. Think of the neighbours.'

Keith assumed his mother was shouting, although he could only see her lips moving. He raised his hand to his ear and stared at her, as if baffled by her entry into the room. Then everything went silent. She had pulled the plug out.

'Mum! You'll ruin that record!'

'It sounds awful anyway. I don't know what you see in Bel Shannon.'

'Why can't you get the names of these pop stars right? You're as bad as Dad.'

Mrs Golder sat down in one of the two tired armchairs, pointing to the other one. Keith slumped into it, wondering what new torment was about to come his way. His mother arranged her dress fussily around her knees and looked at him disapprovingly.

'You really should get some of that hair cut shorter over your ears and collar. I'm surprised the school hasn't written to me.'

Keith lolled back in the armchair and stared at the ceiling, his lips compressed into a grimace of irritation, as his mother went on, 'Mr Davies will employ you every Saturday. You will walk down to the bottom of the road by the Shell garage and he will pick you up in his van at seven o'clock.' She left him no time to butt in or protest. She simply ploughed on, 'He finishes the round at five or six in the evening and will drop you off here outside the house. He'll pay you a pound each Saturday. That's good, Keith, don't you think so, son?'

'Good? It's slave labour! Twelve hours in a freezing van, selling fruit and veg! What do I know about fruit and bloody veg? I don't know one end of a spud from the other.'

'Keith, don't swear! You're only swearing because your father can't hear you. He'd box your ears for you.'

'How generous of him,' muttered Keith, starting to think about crackly green pound notes. Perhaps being driven around the area could be quite good for his image. He would certainly meet a lot of new people, mostly female! How many men queued for spuds, spring onions or mushrooms? This was beginning to sound decidedly more promising. He made a mental note to play 'Running Scared' by Roy Orbison as soon as his mother had finished organising his life.

Seven o'clock on a dark Saturday morning in February was not Keith's idea of the high life. What an unpromising start! He stood on the freezing pavement, his shoes crackling on the ice, his breath surrounding him in clouds, waiting for Mr Davies to arrive. He knew the van quite well. It often stopped at the end of his drive, causing a tailback of traffic, and his mother and her neighbours would go running out of the front door and gather round the back of the van to make their purchases. There was always gossip, and presiding from the interior of the van stood the tall and corpulent figure of Mr Davies, the fruit and veg man. His helper had been Bobby Hughes. Bobby was fourteen, tall and handsome, with a mop of wavy blond hair and a line of cheeky chat for the lady customers. How Keith had hated Bobby! His popularity at school and his prowess on the sports field made Keith fantasise about a dreadful accident befalling him. When he heard Bobby was moving away from the area, he felt quite light-headed with joy. Still, taking over from him with Mr Davies would not be easy. Keith felt he would have to be somehow reborn, transformed into somebody altogether more interesting.

Mr Davies's van was of indeterminate age, and its panels were of different colours and qualities. It might once have been a horsebox. It was hard to tell. The engine sounded more like a steam locomotive, because it hissed and spat as it laboured around the housing estates. At the back was an old brown canvas curtain, which was rolled up and tied to the roof for business, and a low flap, bolted at each side, which was dropped down at each stop.

Just as Keith believed he was on the point of death in the icy blackness, he heard the rattling and lurching of the approaching van. It was five past seven and his working day was about to begin.

Keith's father had commented helpfully, 'At least you don't have to load the van. Mr Davies does all that before he leaves to pick you up. He comes all the way from Wednesbury.'

Keith had the odd feeling that he should somehow feel grateful for this but was not sure why. A man who got up at the crack of dawn to do the sort of day that Mr Davies did must be quite barmy!

The van shuddered to a smoking halt beside him. Should he get into the cab beside Mr Davies? He looked towards the driver for guidance, as the headlights beamed through the thin sleet that was now falling. Mr Davies jerked his thumb towards the back of the vehicle. Keith slithered about trying to haul himself over the rear flap.

'Slide the bolts, you bloody idiot! There's no point trying to climb over the flap. Daft sod!'

Keith did as he was told, whereupon the van abruptly drove off, throwing him onto his back in the darkness, the metal flap banging up and down as if ready to detach itself. Mr Davies turned in the driver's seat and glared through the rectangular aperture behind him into the interior of the van. 'Bolt it up again, you ballerina! What do they teach you at school?'

As he rolled about in the dust, it crossed Keith's mind to tell Mr Davies that none of his lessons covered jumping into a moving van in total darkness. On balance, however, he decided to keep his mouth shut.

It began to get light as the van struggled uphill towards Great Barr, a suburb of north Birmingham. Keith had regained his footing and sat precariously on some bulky sacks, grasping the coarse hessian in both hands to stop himself from flying across to the opposite side and knocking himself out on the metal wall. He wondered whether he would receive any training, since he knew nothing about any of the produce that was beginning to reveal itself to him in the half-light.

Again Mr Davies swivelled in his seat. 'Don't just sit there like Diana Dors! Get to know what you'll be selling. I'll tell you the prices later.' Then he looked up at the rear-view mirror and went on, 'I hope you can add up and count money.'

Keith realised that his mind was completely blank and that he was aware only of the potatoes shifting beneath him and of the exhaust fumes coming up through the rattling wooden floorboards. One detail that Keith did not miss, however, was the large biscuit tin full of packs of ten Senior Service untipped.

The weather gradually improved and the job got easier. By the middle of April Keith had been working with Mr Davies for a couple of months. His day ended in Aldridge, near Walsall, where he lived. The van toured all the housing estates, both private and council. Mr Davies would lurch to a halt at a central point and give several blasts on his hooter. This signal would cause a flurry of activity in the surrounding houses. Down the drives and out of the gates, across the verges and over the pavements, out of the pedestrian alleys and over the playing fields the housewives would flock to Mr Davies's mobile emporium. Some of the ladies were in their twenties, looking glamorous, often with just a dressing gown or overcoat pulled around their nightdress. Others were older and larger, with a rolling gait like a battleship, brandishing empty shopping bags as if they were weapons. Some wore headscarves knotted at the front, revealing vicious-looking steel hairclips. There were ladies with cigarettes in the corner of their mouths, ladies with no teeth and ladies chewing gum. Saturday was the fruit and veg day and Saturdays would not be the same without the big old man in his brown cow gown and faded flat cap.

The added attraction was always Mr Davies's young assistant. In place of Bobby Hughes, the ladies were slowly getting used to Keith Golder, an altogether different figure. Keith was tall and skinny, his brown hair quiffed to look like Elvis. He had a pale sensitive face and surprisingly blue eyes. His patter lacked the joviality of Bobby Hughes, the easy repartee, but he could be darkly sexual, yet with a look of innocence that fascinated the ladies.

The evening sun slanted across Leighswood council estate, bronzing the old van and the gaggle of women gathered around at the back, waiting to be served. Now that Keith was confident in his work, Mr Davies would remain in the driving seat at the front, smoking and barking comments. Keith had grown used to the many insults regularly heaped upon him and hardly flinched nowadays when his head was slapped or a potato bounced off the top of his cranium, ruffling the Elvis Presley hairdo.

'Tell those noisy bloody women to form an orderly queue, you useless streak of nothing!'

Keith strode to the back of the van and stood in the opening, smirking down at the huddle of at least twenty ladies. He cleared his throat.

'Now then, ladies, form a queue please.' His voice faltered a little.

'Queue yourself, gorgeous, and give me a kiss! You can show me your spring onions any time, Keithy!'

Keith breathed deeply to fight back the colour rising in his face. He knew he would be knocking off in an hour. He had not yet pocketed his pack of ten Seniors, he left that until the last minute. He knew it was dishonest but this did not change his behaviour. He did it every week. How could Mr Davies notice? The biscuit tin was a good foot square and the packets were scattered higgledy-piggledy inside.

Then Mr Davies's voice was heard, 'Don't you interfere with my assistant, Mrs Sharpe, or I'll come back there and serve you myself.'

At this remark there was general moaning and Mrs Sharpe piped up again, 'You stay where you are, you old bugger! I can manage very nicely with Keith, thank you. Can't I, Keith?'

'Yes, Mrs Sharpe.'

'Call me Sharon, my darling, and show me what you've got.' She patted her hair to shrieks of raucous laughter.

Keith rattled off his old and new potatoes, spring onions, cabbage, lettuce and the whole litany of produce.

By now Mr Davies had clambered from his seat and made his way aft through the little rectangular hatch into the main part of the van. He glared down at a voluptuous young woman standing next to Mrs Sharpe. Hand on hip, and pouting with her crimson lips, she looked at Mr Davies. He said to her, 'Now then, Myra, I expect you've got some smart comment to make, haven't you?'

Turning away from him she smiled at Keith, licked her lips and purred, 'Do you keep anything really big in your sack, Keith?'

The disorderly queue erupted. Mr Davies said to Keith, 'Get inside and start sweeping the bloody van. I'll deal with this lot.'

So Mr Davies took the orders and repeated them in a loud voice to Keith, who was now hidden in the darkening interior of the van, sweeping furiously and preparing to do the arithmetic. He would scribble feverish calculations on a bunch of brown paper bags.

'Two pound of old and one pound of new, a pound of carrots with no muck on, three Granny Smiths and forty Seniors,' bellowed Mr Davies and then, turning to his customer, he continued, 'What do you think of his suede jacket and winkle-picker shoes, Mrs Perks? Doesn't he look just like a nancy boy?'

'I think he looks very smart, Mr Davies. Perhaps he'd like to bring my stuff to my house for me?'

'No, he wouldn't. He hasn't got time to run errands for the likes of you. I pay him to work.'

'Pity,' mumbled Mrs Perks.

'Never mind pity! That will be fourteen shillings and ten pence to you and you can take it home your blooming self!'

Then it was the turn of Beryl Lees, with her bouffonned hair and drainpipe jeans. She stood by the back of the van and looked up at Mr Davies. 'Ask Keith if he knows "Will You Love Me Tomorrow?" by the Shirelles.'

'I'll do no such thing, Beryl. Give your order and sod off! I've had a long day and I don't wish to discuss popular music with you.'

'Twenty fags and two pound of new potatoes and I wasn't talking to you anyway, so put that in your pipe and smoke it!'

Mr Davies turned to Keith. 'Sadly, Keith, in order to make a living, we have to serve the likes of Beryl here. So do her spuds and her fags, then carry on sweeping.' He turned to Beryl. 'Five and sixpence, Beryl, and don't ask me to change that ten bob note.'

In a little over an hour Keith was jumping off the back of the van at the top of his drive. Mr Davies refused to stop the van, so Keith had to take his chances, with a queue of traffic behind, jumping out while the van rolled at a good running pace. Mr Davies had given him his pound note and had assured him, as usual, that he was a complete waste of money and had better be on time next Saturday. Keith patted the ten Senior Service in his pocket as he trotted towards his front door.

Keith's sister, Peggy, was in her first year at the grammar school. The largest part of little Peggy's body was her mouth. She had a strikingly loud voice and was not slow to use it. Keith sauntered into the lounge to find Peggy kneeling at the Dansette de Luxe, doing a sort of hand jive and singing to Elvis's 'His Latest Flame' in a deafening but wholly tuneless voice.

'Push off, Keith, I'm sorry you've finished work. Did you steal any more fags?'

'Fizz up and bust! Has your new boyfriend snogged you yet?'

Peggy stood up and beamed at Keith. 'Yes, he did actually.'

Keith leaned forward and peered closely at her face. He pointed at her mouth, 'So he didn't mind that lump of food stuck between your two front teeth?'

Peggy dashed to the mirror, muttering that she wouldn't fall for that sort of trick. She raised her upper lip and stared in the mirror, her eyes widening in horror.

'Oh shit! He must have noticed!'

'Well, he was obviously too sex-starved to worry,' drawled Keith as he adopted an Elvis pose.

It was at that point that Mrs Golder swept into the little room. She gave Peggy's backside a loud slap. 'I heard that language, Peggy. Get upstairs and tidy your room.' Keith started to laugh but was cut short by his mother, who rounded on him: 'And you can shut up too. I won't have talk about sex in this house. Your sister is only twelve. Don't think just because you're earning your keep at the moment you can do as you please. Do some homework and get from under my feet!'

In the July heat the van was like an oven. As it jolted and bounced its way towards its next port of call, Keith tried to light a cigarette, braced against the sacks and boxes. In spite of the heat, Mr Davies sat in his cab with his flat cap and brown cow gown on, a cigarette smouldering in the corner of his mouth. Each time he shifted the gears, Keith was pitched several feet forward. The interior was filled with a thick cocktail of apples, tomatoes and exhaust fumes.

This Saturday was Keith's last day on the fruit and veg round. Neither he nor Mr Davies had mentioned it, though both were aware of it. Mr Davies had not thrown a single potato at Keith today, nor had he called him a milk sop, a cissy or a nancy.

Mr Davies turned the van round in a cul-de-sac that was their normal 3 p.m. stopping place. Now the van was parked facing the way out. He switched the engine off and for a few brief seconds there was silence. Then Mr Davies gave several toots on the horn. Keith jumped down into the road and trotted across the grassed space to knock on the doors shouting, 'Fruit and veg! Get your fruit and veg!' Then, trotting back to the van, he started to relight the remains of his cigarette.

Clumping along inside the van, Mr Davies grumbled, 'You can stub that out as soon as you like. Get ready to receive customers.'

Keith took the cigarette end and placed it behind his ear, whereupon Mr Davies bent forward, seized it and threw it into the road. He then slapped Keith's ear. 'We sell food here, you idiot, and that doesn't give a hygienic image!'

Keith rubbed his ear and said, 'But I've seen you smoking while you serve customers, Mr D.'

He cowered as another slap landed on him.

'We'll have less cheeky comments and more work, if you please!'

A group of ladies was forming around the back of the van, plonking their baskets and bags on the dusty floorboards, which were about level with their bosoms. A large, round lady with

18

corrugated hair and thick glasses beamed at Keith: 'Last day, eh, Keefy? Are you sad to be leaving me, you sexy thing?'

Keith stared at her, all eighteen stone of her or more, and stammered, 'Er, hello Mrs Osborne, I er...'

Mr Davies appeared from the dark recess of the van, reached down, pushed Keith aside and glared. 'You order your goods, Mrs Osborne. Never mind sexy. I'll give you bloody sexy!'

'That you won't!' gobbled Mrs Osborne, her whiskery chins quaking indignantly.

Keith began to realise that a goodbye kiss would be expected here and tried to think about the evening ahead, especially *Hancock's Half Hour* on the telly.

He was right. Once laden with her goods, Mrs Osborne said to Keith, 'Here's the money, Keefy, and I'll have a big kiss in exchange for it. And before you kiss me, I want you to say, "This is for you, Dora."'

Keith thought of England and did the deed and it wasn't until they were on their way to Aldridge for him to get off that Mr Davies said, 'Well done with Mrs Osborne, lad. You did well there.' Keith was sure he saw tears in the old man's eyes.

The whole experience of the fruit and veg round was coming to an end. Keith would be in the fourth year in September and his parents insisted he must study hard from then on for his O levels. The summer holidays started next week and Mr Davies would be chugging around the housing estates without him. Keith stood in the opening just behind the cab, talking to Mr Davies, who was seated slightly below him at the wheel with over an inch of ash clinging to his cigarette end.

'So what's the new boy like, Keith?'

'His name is Charlie, same age as me and he's all right.'

'Is he normal or is he as daft as you?'

'About the same. He'll be waiting at the same place at seven next Saturday.'

Mr Davies stared ahead, swinging the steering wheel this way and that in the drowsy evening sunshine. Keith realised all at once how much he would miss it all. The van ground to a smoky halt outside Keith's house. That was unusual for a start. He usually had to jump for his life to get off. Mr Davies climbed out of the cab, leaving the engine running, and extended his right hand to Keith. They stood together on the bright pavement, feeling the heat from the bonnet and ignoring the build-up of traffic behind the van.

'Did you bolt up the flap, son?'

'Yes, and I've totalled the cash and bagged it up.'

Mr Davies cleared his throat as they shook hands. Keith was overwhelmed to be treated like a man outside his own house.

'Well, good luck, son, and don't forget your Seniors.' He thrust a packet of ten at Keith, who hesitated, looking up at Mr Davies's face.

'What are these for, Mr D?'

Mr Davies smiled a knowing smile and placed a large, beefy hand on Keith's shoulder. 'You know bloody well what they're for, you cheeky sod! Those there are your weekly perk.'

Keith smiled at him, glanced down and walked away down the drive to his front door. He heard the familiar sound of the old van puffing away towards Wednesbury.

Stair-rods. We used to call rain like that stair-rods. Wood Green Road was barely visible in the greyness and the spray from the traffic. Wednesbury in the rain was even more depressing than Wednesbury in the sunshine, or so it seemed to Glyn. From the tall windows of the student common room the deluge could be seen puddling the cramped staff car park. It drummed against the side of the building and on the roofs of the cars, forming a sort of mist just above the surface of the road. Glyn stood on the hot-water pipe that ran just above the floor and used the back of his hand to clear a big circle in the condensation. Even as he watched, the circle began to collapse as drops of moisture slid in rivulets down to the red tiled window sill. He wiped his wet hand on the backside of his trousers and puffed out a sigh, noticing that the buses were already lit up inside and some of the cars had their little round sidelights on.

At eighteen years of age, boredom is a serious business. A youth like Glyn has no way of pacing himself, and Glyn was convinced that it would rain for ever. His two years at the College of Further Education were drawing to a close. In two or three weeks' time he would be sitting his A levels and then going up to university.

At over six feet tall he had no reason to stand on the hot water pipe, it was just something you did. The cream paint was covered in black shoe prints. He looked at his Timex. Three o'clock. Where was she? This rain must have delayed her bus. At this moment he was the only person in the common room and could afford to move around between the chairs, huffing and puffing and throwing his arms up in frustration.

His display was cut short when Judy knocked the door open with her hip, her arms laden with books. She looked at Glyn, rolled her eyes and dumped her books on the side table among all the duffel bags and satchels. Her face took on a more mischievous expression as she applied a match to her Consulate ('cool as a mountain stream') and collapsed into an armchair that had seen far better days.

'Waiting for your girlfriend, Glyn? Of course, it's Thursday, when she comes for her lesson with Mr Newbold. O level Latin! Jeez, she must be mad!'

'Why is everybody so interested in my personal life?' grunted Glyn, fitting his favourite single on the turntable. Judy inhaled mentholated smoke as the opening guitar riff of 'The Last Time' by the Rolling Stones filled the room.

'You know I hate the Stones. Give me Dave Clark any day.'

'That's why I put the Stones on,' Glyn replied sourly, returning to the big wet window to see whether the rain had stopped. The rain had not stopped.

In the summer of 1964 Glyn Phipps was eighteen. He was tall but not *that* tall, he was good looking but not *that* good looking and he was bright but not *that* bright. He was a serious, hard-working A-level student from quite an ordinary background. His father was a clerk at the Inland Revenue and his mother was a housewife. His father drove into Birmingham in an ancient Morris shooting brake and his mother hoovered the threadbare carpets and produced meals from cheap cuts of meat. Ever since he had turned sixteen, Glyn had been taller than both his parents and showed his awareness of this by smoking in the house. His sister, Barbara, told him he was pretentious and he scoffed at her, because he had no idea what the word meant. He was starting to wear out his buckled shoes along the outer edges because of his new way of walking, slightly bow-legged. He had also begun to make a sort of chewing movement with his mouth as he walked. This was to simulate chewing gum but without all the inconvenience. He had tried hooking his thumbs in his trouser pockets as he walked but had discovered that it made his arms ache. His aim was to be a nice sort of chap but to resemble an East End thug if at all possible. He did quite well with the girls at college, although he had never mastered the skill of chatting casually with a cigarette smouldering in the corner of his mouth.

It was a James Dean thing that he rather liked. He always found he had to screw up one eye and fight back a bout of coughing. He wished he was heavier. During the changeover between lectures, if he were jostled in the crush on the stairs or in the corridor, he might end up thrown against the wall, his arms flailing, not a desirable spectacle when trying to strike a pose.

So why was Glyn Phipps doing his A-level studies at college rather than in the sixth form at his local grammar school? Well, his need to be an individual had not endeared him to his teachers and his father had judged it best that he should leave and start afresh for his A levels.

It was during the run-up to the start of the exams that Glyn had seen the girl. On Mondays and Thursdays she would step from the platform of the Walsall bus in her green uniform and grey felt hat. She did two hours of O level Latin a week with Mr Newbold, one of the language teachers. He had a hairy nose, smoked a pipe and called all male students 'laddie'.

The girl was quite small with very dark hair cut in a bob and flicked forward at the sides, very Cilla Black. In spite of her school uniform, Glyn beheld a goddess. She walked with a sway and a self-awareness which made him feel quite short of breath. He had watched her from the common-room window, inspecting her face, which was delicate, like a doll's, yet with just a hint of make-up, Glyn felt sure. She carried her books in a little brown briefcase, almost like a little picnic case with a handle and reinforced corners. He watched her leave at half past four each time, with a sway and a twitch, tossing her head back and letting the wind blow her hair around, her grey felt hat dangling from her tiny hand. Glyn thought, I have got to meet that girl.

His mistake, however, was to share his enthusiasm with most of the common room.

At lunchtimes, when the common room was heaving with students and the air was fogged with cigarette smoke, crowing male voices would ask, 'Got off with her yet, Phippsy?'

'Like to shag a fifth-former, would you, Glyn?'

The dilemma for Glyn was that the girl of his dreams spent scarcely more than two hours a week on the premises. As Glyn scanned the crowded room, listening to the noise of conversation, he felt a growing sense of impatience with himself. All he had done so far was to watch her arrive and leave. He had stood at the window like an abandoned poodle, almost revelling in an overwhelming sense of helplessness. His own credibility was at stake here: Glyn Phipps, the smoothie, The Saint, the charmer. He realised with a jolt that he did not even know her name. He looked out of the corner of his eye at his friend Martyn, sprawled in an old armchair with his girlfriend of no more than one week sitting in his lap, sharing his cigarette and showing her knickers. Glyn thought, everything comes easy for other people. Why do I have to go through so much for a few ordinary pleasures?

Martyn's girlfriend turned to Glyn, as she struggled to close her legs. Glyn pretended to be unaware that she wanted to speak to him. He felt people should have to make an effort to win his attention.

'Glyn, Martyn tells me you fancy Cherry, who comes here for Latin?'

Glyn trusted he had successfully camouflaged his sharp intake of breath. 'Fancy who?'

'Whom,' sneered Martyn, fondling his girlfriend's left breast, 'it should be whom and not who.'

Glyn looked at Martyn, then at the girl. 'Okay, fancy whom?'

'Fancy Cherry. I used to be at school with her. Do you want me to fix you up?' She casually brushed aside Martyn's furtive hand and lowered her eyelids at Glyn.

Glyn examined his fingernails nonchalantly. 'No thank you, I'm quite capable of getting my own girlfriend.'

'Of course you are, Phippsy, that's why you haven't got one at the moment.' Glyn considered suggesting that Martyn should get stuffed but didn't like to say it in front of his new girlfriend.

The main entrance to the college was quite imposing in a modern post-war kind of way. There were half a dozen concrete steps leading up to a heavy swing door and a spacious foyer with a parquet floor and reception window on the left. Straight ahead a flight of stairs led to the two upper floors. On a Monday afternoon Glyn had two hours of English Literature. He was marooned in an upstairs classroom which looked over a few parked cars, a row of bins, a wooden fence and then a housing estate. Much as he enjoyed his session with Mr Milner and eleven other students, he really wanted to race down the stairs at three o'clock to welcome Cherry to the building and to introduce himself, the teenage equivalent of Roger Moore or Sean Connery. The alternative was to wait until Thursday afternoon when he had a free period and would usually gawp out of the common-room window to watch the gorgeous girl mincing towards the steps, her green pleated skirt blowing tantalisingly around her black stockings. So it was during a class discussion about the Prologue to Chaucer's *Canterbury Tales* that Glyn decided to force matters forward a little.

'Mr Milner, would you mind if I go to the toilet?'

'Of course, Glyn. Clearly your bladder is influencing you more strongly than Geoffrey Chaucer.'

Then a male voice piped up, 'Let's hope it is his bladder and not something smellier!'

'Thank you very much, Master Townsend,' said the teacher, and turning to Glyn, 'Yes, you may go.'

It was five minutes to three. Glyn bounded down the first few stairs, then checked himself. What if Cherry came through the entrance and saw him *running*? He changed to a peculiar style of swagger and adopted a sneer. He ruffled his hair a little, but not too much, and cleared his throat so that his voice could be pitched deeper. By the time he reached the foot of the stairs, he had twice narrowly avoided spraining his ankle. His aim was to bump into Cherry as if by accident, while he was walking from one side of the foyer to the other. This necessitated his walking repeatedly up and down the foyer, squinting sideways towards the swing door. Blast! he thought, where the hell is she?

A hand slid the glass of the reception window upwards and a middle-aged lady poked her face through the gap: 'Are you all right, Glyn? You seem to be lost. Are you waiting for someone?'

'No, Mrs Anderson, just thinking.' The face withdrew and the window banged shut. Then, through the glass of the swing door, Glyn saw Cherry.

He walked towards her, his fingers playing nervously around his black turtle-neck top, which he was convinced gave him the moody look of the taller of the two Righteous Brothers. Cherry looked up at him and, clasping her little case to her chest, said, 'Hello, are you my reception committee today?'

Glyn laughed awkwardly and swallowed. She was even prettier close to than when seen through the common-room window.

'What? I, er, no, I just happened to be going to the toi... just happened to be passing.' God! How pathetic! Also, he was forgetting to pitch his voice a lot lower. He tried again.

'Hello, you must be Cherry. My name is Glyn.' That sounded better. He extended his hand for a formal handshake, then took it away again and scratched the side of his face awkwardly. Cherry smiled up at him. She was calm and poised with just a little hint of make-up and perfectly arched eyebrows. He smelt her perfume and felt quite dizzy. She seemed mildly amused by him, which was not quite the effect Glyn had hoped for.

Glyn racked his brains and came up with, 'Can I take you to the Latin classroom?' Now she actually laughed at him.

'My, my, Glyn, you have been doing your homework, haven't you? You know my name and you know why I'm here. I'm very flattered.'

Glyn felt things were going better and better. He gave a cocky smile and ran a hand through his hair, struggling not to think about how Cherry would look naked in front of him.

'Come on, I'll take you there anyway.' He took her gently by the elbow and led her along the corridor to Mr Newbold's room. She was Mr Newbold's only student for that session and, as they entered his classroom, there he was, sprawling at his desk, his unlit pipe in his mouth. He stood up to greet his student.

'Here again, Cherry! Pull up a seat by me.' He peered over the top of his reading glasses and, looking at Glyn, said, 'Don't you have a lecture to attend, laddie?'

'Er, yes, Mr Newbold. I just brought Cherry.'

Mr Newbold removed his pipe from between his teeth, continued to eye Glyn up and down and muttered, 'Laddie, Cherry knows the way here full well. She's been coming here regularly.'

Glyn began to feel uncomfortable, until Cherry quickly squeezed his hand surreptitiously and said to Mr Newbold, 'Glyn was very helpful actually, Mr Newbold, I wish all the boys were as kind as he is.'

Glyn floated on a cloud of euphoria, only matched by his level of arousal. He would have liked to remove all of Cherry's clothing there and then.

Mr Newbold appeared now to see Glyn in a new and more favourable light: 'Well, thank you, laddie, now clear off to your lecture.'

Just as it was inevitable that Glyn would ask Cherry to go out with him, so it was equally inevitable that she would accept. Glyn was captivated by her. He would parade her along the pavement of Park Street in Walsall on a warm Saturday night, looking to left and right to see who was eyeing the pair of them. He would either drape his arm casually around her shoulders, so that he looked rather like a drunk, or he would place it more demurely around her waist, making it difficult for him to walk, because she was so much shorter than he. Their conversation was stilted and giggly at first, neither being sure what to talk about. Glyn learned slowly how to relax a little more and be himself. Cherry, in contrast, was always a picture of self-confidence, never saying too much or too little and, from Glyn's point of view, always looking perfect.

Glyn was convinced that Cherry must be proud to be seen with him in the street. There couldn't be many other boys she could choose who would cut such a dash. He was a college boy, not a schoolboy, and a good catch for a sixteen-year-old schoolgirl from the Beechdale Estate. He lived in this fool's paradise until mid-August, when all his exams were over and he was set to go to Manchester University in October.

It was very dark and it had rained. They had had two indifferent coffees at the Del Rio coffee bar halfway up Bradford Street. Now they were down a narrow unpaved alley with puddles at their feet, a dilapidated latticework wooden fence in front of them and a wall behind, which Glyn was leaning on. Glyn didn't like Walsall but it was convenient for Cherry. Raindrops dripped into Glyn's hair and down the back of his neck from the tangle of briars above the wall. Glyn was holding Cherry to him, and they were surrounded by a cloud of their intermingled breath.

Cherry looked up into his eyes. Glyn assumed she was overcome by lust for him but to his surprise she whispered, 'You don't kiss very well, do you, Glyn?' Glyn was dumbstruck. No girl had ever criticised him in this way before. As he gaped at her, wounded, she added, laughing at him, 'Most boys do that tongue thing. You don't.'

'What tongue thing?' Glyn was ever so slightly needled.

Cherry stood on tiptoe, leaning towards him and still laughing, 'Here, let me show you.'

Glyn's arms flailed about and he feared he might choke to death. This was a revelation to him and he would need time to get used to it. As a reflex response, he coughed slightly.

'Yuk! That's disgusting, Glyn!' That was the first signpost that Glyn failed to read.

The second came at the party. Cherry's school friend, Pauline, was seventeen years old and was throwing a lavish party. It was September and a Saturday evening. Cherry and Pauline had just started in the sixth form at their school but Glyn was still at leisure, having attained the A-level results he wanted. He would soon be going up to Manchester University, as he kept reminding Cherry. Even Glyn was not clear whether it was out of pride or the need to provoke some sort of reaction from Cherry.

The evening was damp and clammy. The house looked quite imposing, with lights on in every room, loud music and excited voices. Pauline greeted them at the door, holding a glass of something. Glyn noticed she was swaying slightly and her eyes were abnormally bright. She showed them inside and invited them to help themselves to a drink from the kitchen. Cherry plonked herself in a leatherette armchair and despatched Glyn to get her a Martini Rosso and a beer for himself. When Glyn reappeared, she patted the arm of the chair for him to sit on, then rapidly placed her upturned hand on it, so that he would sit on her hand. Balancing the drinks as if he were some kind of skilled acrobatic performer, he lowered himself towards the arm of the chair. Then, as if stung, he straightened up abruptly, the drinks spilling over both his hands.

'What the hell was that?' He turned to find Cherry laughing at him.

'My hand, you prudish boy!'

'Why did you do that? Look what's happened to the bloody drinks!'

If Glyn had looked carefully at Cherry, he would have realised she felt rather foolish now and no little embarrassed. People were looking at them both, some of them pausing in mid-snog to laugh at them.

Cherry looked up at Glyn. 'I thought you'd like it, most boys would.'

Glyn guessed he was irresistible to Cherry but felt this was going a little too far. He was unused to the predatory female. The girls he had known so far simply sat like dummies while he thrust his hand inside their blouse.

One Sunday afternoon, as they were strolling in the weak autumn sunshine that dappled the lawns of Walsall Arboretum, Glyn had become uncharacteristically passionate and animated. He turned to Cherry and took her by both shoulders while they were both in mid-stride: 'Come and live with me in Manchester. We could get a student flat.'

29

'Glyn, I'm doing my A-level work and I've got two years of sixth form to do. What am I supposed to do in Manchester?'

Glyn's face fell and his shoulders sagged. He had just assumed that Cherry would go anywhere with him.

'You could go to a local school.' He felt sure he could bring her round. It was unthinkable that she could be tempted to go with any other boy after him. He knew other boys looked at her but he was fairly sure she didn't look back at them. Why would she?

Glyn stood in the cinema queue with three of his friends. He was the only one of the four of them who had a girlfriend at the moment and he was eager to show her off. The Savoy cinema stood at Townend at the top of Park Street in Walsall. Its elevated position made it a sort of magnet for wind and rain. The huddled queue, a mass of shiny, wet umbrellas, dripping trilbies and upturned collars extended round the corner to the side of the building. A raw wind bearing fits of rain pinned the queue against the wall and everyone waited impatiently for some forward movement towards the warmth and the dryness.

Glyn and his friends had fallen silent and stood tugging their collars as high up their necks as possible. Glyn had been brimming with confidence, thinking how impressed his friends would be to see Cherry in her tight jeans and white roll-neck jumper, smoking in the way that only a sexy girl can smoke. She would draw on her cigarette, the red tip glowing like a meteor, then hold it away from her as she inhaled with a hiss Glyn thought would never end. Finally, her eyes closed into slits, she would release a thin jet of smoke, her lips set in an almost perfectly circular pout. Sometimes she would offer the cigarette to Glyn, who would then derive erotic satisfaction from closing his mouth over the lipstick traces on the filter tip.

She was late. It was after seven. A tiny nagging doubt began to grow in Glyn's head and in his stomach but it was far in the background. She only lived up the road. It was just a few minutes on the bus.

30

'Where is this bird then, Glyn? I think she's just a figment of your imagination.'

'Yeah, where is she, Phippsy? I've heard she's a bit of all right. What does she see in you?'

Glyn laughed good-humouredly in the cold rain. In his own mind there was no need for any justification. That was why Cherry had gone on about rubber johnnies. During recent weeks she had even pointed out places where he might buy them. Glyn did not take this too seriously. It was just her way of emphasising how she felt towards him. October, the month of his departure to university, loomed ever nearer. Glyn reckoned this must be a major worry for Cherry.

By twenty past seven the queue was shuffling forward and there was still no Cherry. Glyn was mortified. He was angry because he looked foolish. His clothes were soaking wet and he certainly would not go into the cinema without Cherry. He told his friends as much.

'Nice try, Phippsy! You almost had me believing she was going out with you.'

Glyn was too downhearted to be defiant. Fortunately for him his face was already wet with rain, otherwise he would have drawn even more ridicule.

Within twenty minutes he was jumping off the bus and trotting towards Cherry's front door. In two strides he had covered the short pathway and was tapping desperately to attract attention. The house was in darkness and there was no reply. By now Glyn was very wet indeed. He had to get to Pauline's. She would know what was going on. That would mean another walk and a ride on the Leamore bus. But, Glyn reflected, what else had he got to do? The evening had turned out to be a nightmare rather than the triumph he had planned, in which he was to have been the centre of attention, his pretty girlfriend clinging to his arm and smiling at his friends. It was just bloody typical how things seemed to work out! This sort of thing never happened to James Bond or John Steed.

Pauline's door opened to the sound of washing up and the *Z-Cars* theme. Glyn beheld a very different Pauline from the party girl who had greeted him previously. Her face was pale, her freckles were more prominent and her long, brown hair was lank. Her green eyes were filled with concern and her hands fluttered about in front of her, as if seeking a place to rest. Glyn thought it odd that she did not invite him inside and she spoke to him almost in a whisper.

'Well, you must know where she is, Pauline.' Glyn was aware that there was a catch in his voice and he was surprised to realise that he was close to tears.

'Go home, Glyn. I expect she will get in touch.'

'You do know where she is, don't you?'

Pauline nodded and whispered, 'She's here.' There was a pause as Glyn's mouth fell open. Pauline added, 'But she doesn't want to see you.'

Baffled, Glyn stood on tiptoe, trying to see into the hall-way over Pauline's shoulder. He called Cherry's name, and then called it again.

Pauline pulled the door to, so that they were both standing outside. 'I told you to go home, Glyn. Now go. Cherry is upset and I don't want you to make things even worse.'

Then from inside the house came a male voice, as the front door opened a crack. 'For God's sake come inside, Pauline, and don't make a spectacle on the front doorstep. Whoever that is, send them away.'

What shocked Glyn most was his own sense of loss. This was a sensation which was quite new to him and he saw clearly now that his silly idea of some sort of balance of power between himself and Cherry was a complete nonsense. How many times had he read on his school report, 'Could try harder'?

When the letter came, Glyn opened it far more nervously than he had opened his A-level results. His stomach was floating inside his body and he felt his breath grow shallow. He withdrew the letter from the envelope and recognised Cherry's large round hand and her light blue ink. He recognised the way in which she dotted her 'i's with circles rather than blobs and he saw that she had called him 'Glyn' rather than 'G', which had been her pet name for him. His eyes prickled with tears as he read:

Dear Glyn,

I cannot go out with you any more and this is leading nowhere. It has been over two months and still we have not done it. I made it clear enough at least I thought I did. But you were always in a world of your own. It's not what I'm used to. You are a very nice boy and I am very fond of you but I want a man and not a boy and you are not yet a man. I know you will be very successful in your life and wish you luck at university.

Really sorry,

Cherry

Glyn's eyes filled and his world wobbled in front of him.

Does the sun shine through the leaves,
Nettles nodding in the breeze?
Does the rutted field smell warm,
Children wandering without harm?
Endless days to while away,
Nothing much to do or say,
Running wild down tracks and lanes,
Life will never seem the same.

It was a dreamy summer's day. One of those days when anything could happen. It was a day on which older people sat dozing, dogs lay sprawled in doorways and the only sound was the murmuring of flies. The air was as heavy as syrup. It smelt of dry grass, lawn cuttings and rose bushes. The heat shimmered over the rooftops of Redhouse council estate. The streets were quiet. There was no traffic. No one seemed to want to go anywhere.

But if you listened very carefully, you could hear voices coming from the side entrance of one of the redbrick semis. The voices were shrill and excited and there was a rattling of bicycles being moved from their resting place against the shady wall. Those were boys' voices, boys who wanted to be on the move, who wanted to feel the warm air blowing in their faces and through their clothes. The boys had grown impatient as, one by one, the grown-ups had dozed off, their heads on one side, a newspaper in their lap, the football commentator muttering softly as *Sportsview* with Peter Dimmock heated the little television sets.

They pushed their bikes to the wrought-iron garden gate and heard it clatter shut on its spring as they swung their legs over the saddles and pushed down on the pedals. The little gardens swished by. The boys did not speak, but now and then the one at the front would look round and smile. On the main Walsall Road it was strictly single file and all the tomfoolery had to stop.

The boys felt the hot draught from passing buses, motorbikes with sidecars and lorries whining in low gear, struggling with sacks of coal.

Col watched his friend Graham's legs pumping up and down like pistons, his short trousers flapping, one sock up and one sock down. Col was jealous of his friend's bike with its many cogs and gears and its fancy drinking bottle on the handlebars. But he liked Graham, whose dad was a charge hand and therefore quite posh. Col's dad was a drayman who rolled barrels about. He had big muscles but quite a small pay packet. Graham's dad wore a cow gown over a shirt and tie. Col's dad wore a vest and a flat cap.

After they had turned right off the main road and were heading towards Rushall, Graham saw Col take a packet of cigarettes from his trouser pocket and expertly tap one, filter first, into his mouth. Then, riding with no hands, he cupped his hands to his mouth and lit up. Graham caught a whiff of Park Drive. He wondered whether Col had forgotten him but didn't care too much. He didn't like smoking. He liked Colin because he knew about things, he was wise beyond his years and had the kind of canny smile which made him look much older. He sometimes patted Graham on the shoulder and called him 'old son'. He wasn't sure why Colin liked him, though. Colin was a popular boy and could go on a bike ride with lots of other people. Not that Graham was a loner, in fact people liked him, but for a different reason. Graham was a sensitive boy who read a lot and watched *Robinson Crusoe* on television. He was far less rugged than Colin but he had a growing lanky grace about him. Colin was destined to be a thickset man in later years but for the time being, at eleven years of age, he just seemed a tough guy to Graham.

They both cycled as close to the verge as they could, so as to let the grass stroke their calves and knees as they rode. Col would actually cycle onto the grass and stick his knees out in a bow-legged kind of way to make Graham laugh. Graham rode up alongside him, because the road was deserted, and roared with laughter to see him pull a face like a chimp with the cigarette pointing upwards towards his nostrils.

When they stopped, it was as if an unseen signal had been given, it just happened. Colin jumped off his bike and dropped it flat in the grass, announcing that he needed what he called 'a slash'. Graham assumed he would walk off to a private place to be hidden from view but no, Colin simply turned his back and asked Graham, 'What do you want to be when you grow up?' Fascinated, Graham watched the pale amber stream spring forth from Colin and patter into the grass, causing a cloud of midges to rise into the sunlight.

'Don't know. I think I'd like to be a spaceman. I'd like to go to Mars.' Graham half-hoped Col would turn before he tucked himself in, just out of curiosity, but he didn't.

'My dad wants me to be a drayman like him. He says it's steady work.'

They remounted and rode on without a word, until Linley Wood appeared ahead on their right. When they reached the wood, they dismounted and walked with their bikes into the green twilight. It was like a cathedral with a tall, green vault that filtered the sunlight and let it fall in a sparkling mosaic on the cracked clay floor. They trod softly and spoke in a whisper, looking around them in awe. It was cool and silent. The woodland path was well worn and ran up and downhill, past huge fallen trunks, thickets of holly and tall tangles of briar.

'There's a field ahead where we can rest,' whispered Col, although neither of them felt weary. Sometimes resting seems to children to be something they ought to do, because it's what adults do. Resting can seem quite grown up.

They emerged into sunlight, propped their bikes against a giant oak, took a run to leap across a narrow ditch and stepped into a cornfield with golden ears taller than their own. The idea that they were invisible filled them with delight, as they ran through the corn with their arms outstretched, the tall dry stalks bobbing into their faces. After a few minutes Col fell flat on his back on the ground and stretched out his arms and legs like a starfish. The smell of damp straw rose all around them. Graham sank to his knees and looked at his friend. Col clasped his hands behind his head, screwed up his face with concentration and asked, 'What does a spaceman do?'

'I don't know, goes into space and visits planets.'

'Sounds bloody boring to me,' laughed Col, breaking off a stalk which he used to poke Graham in the throat. Graham leaned forward and pinned his friend down by the shoulders but his arms gave way and he fell on top of him. They looked at each other, as the laughing stopped quite abruptly. They stayed in that position for several seconds, motionless.

Then Graham pulled away and sat up beside his friend. Without looking at him, he asked, 'Have you ever had a girlfriend, Col?'

Col frowned, as if the question was a really difficult one: 'Not really. Never had the time. When you have a bike, you just don't have time for girls. Have you had one?'

'No, I never really thought much about it.'

'But you thought about it just now. Why was that?'

The conversation stalled, as they looked at each other, wondering what came next. Even time seemed to hold its breath. Graham was quite surprised at some of the things going through his head.

'Do you want to go yet?' asked Col.

'No.'

Long into the golden afternoon they sat, as the world rolled slowly into dusk. Graham had taken his shirt off and had spread it under him. When at length he stood up on tiptoe, trying to see above the ocean of corn, Col watched him appraisingly. He took in the square, knobbly shoulders and straight, white back. He realised he was lost for words, so he said nothing. When Graham sat down again, Col patted him on the shoulder and then withdrew his hand as if burnt, finding his friend's skin was surprisingly warm, although the afternoon had grown cooler.

'Do you want to go back now, old son?' asked Col, watching Graham, now on his feet again, struggling with his shirt. He realised his voice had caught slightly and he cleared his throat softly.

'I think we should,' Graham smiled down at his friend, with the odd realisation that he was somehow in control at this moment. Was it just because he was standing and Col was still sitting? No, it was something else, something he was quite unable to put into thoughts, let alone words. He held out his hand and Colin took it. Graham pulled him up to his feet. They stood and faced each other, their faces lit by the low sun, the endless corn stretching away in every direction.

They cycled home in silence, their strange, long shadows running ahead of them. No word was exchanged but now and then they would ride side by side and smile at each other, both aware that a bridge had been crossed and that they had taken several steps on their passage to the future and into the awareness of manhood.

THE DRAMA QUEEN

33, Harborough Road,
Walsall,
Staffs.

18th August 1965

Dear Viv,

I'm writing just to let you know I shall be on my way to Leeds University in a few days, to take up my post as lecturer in the English Department.

I realise you may not even want to know what I'm doing now since we finished and you chucked me. I know you will soon be going up to university, though I don't know which one. You hadn't decided when I last saw you.

We had two good years in spite of the age gap between us and maybe at a future time you will give us another chance.

My address in Leeds will be 9, Brudenell Avenue, Leeds 6, W. Yorks. I hope you will drop me a line.

Yours,

Cliff

I folded Cliff's letter carefully along the existing creases and popped it into my shoulder bag, feeling more like Mata Hari than simply Cliff's ex. It was true, I had chucked him in a fit of pique. He was so adamant that I'd go for Birmingham University, so as to continue living at home with my parents, the cushy option. Little did he know! He really believed that only material things motivated me. It must be an impression I give to all my boyfriends – though you could hardly call Cliff a boy. He was a war baby.

Now here I am, sitting in Ken's Standard Pennant on the verge, listening to the rain on the roof. He's been gone about ten minutes with his four-and-a-half-gallon jerry can. He'll be soaked to the skin by the time he gets to Guymer's Garage, the Esso on the way to Barr Beacon.

He was furious when the car ran out of petrol. I'd never heard him say 'fuck' before. He seemed the ultimate smoothie, his clothes, his way of talking, his carefully casual hair. He's a bit like Dave Clark but taller and skinnier and he wears those white roll-neck jumper things that make you look as if you've got no neck.

Don't get me wrong, I do like him. So do lots of other girls. That's why I stick around partly. Cliff had a Honda 50 motor scooter thing and I used to freeze to death on it. I could never wear this skirt on it – I nearly always had to wear jeans or trousers when we went out.

Anyway, it's the bloke that matters, not the mode of transport. At least that's what a nice sort of girl would say, whether she believed it or not. But you know, being comfortable is important. Cliff would always ask, 'Are you comfortable, Viv? All right, Viv?'

On the other hand Ken goes, 'How do I look with my hair like this, Viv? Do you think I look fanciable in this, Viv?'

Sadly, the truth is that Ken would look fanciable in a brown paper bag. He doesn't need to try as hard as he does but it's best he stays in the dark about that.

I first met Ken three months ago as I was coming out of the library at Moat House. I had planned to cross the road and sit on the grass in the Croft to do some reading about Jean-Paul Sartre for my university interview. The idea of reading about Existentialism while sitting under a big chestnut tree appealed to me. It was while I was gathering my books under my arm that this bloke in a Standard Pennant swept into the car park and all but knocked me over.

'Hi! Need a lift anywhere?'

'But I don't even know you.'

'Ken,' he said, slightly puzzled, as if his identity should be obvious.

'I don't think I know you, Ken.'

'No, but I know you – Vivienne Whitehouse. You were in the third year at the grammar school when I was doing A levels. Surprised you don't remember me, Kenneth Whale. I was the drummer in the school group, the Savages.'

So, Ken drove me home and he drove me to a lot of other places too. He wasn't the sort of bloke you could put off or turn down. Ken spoilt me, he spent money on me, bought me clothes and took me to nice restaurants. This was very different from life with Cliff, although I must admit Ken expected a lot more in return than Cliff had ever asked for, if you get my drift. He told me his nickname was Choker, because he always shovelled his food down and occasionally had a bad choking fit as a result. Ken just assumed I'd become his property and that there was an understanding between us about certain things. While we were driving along in his car he would put his hand up my skirt and touch the inside of my thigh while continuing to talk about his good chances of promotion at work. You know the way you show your holiday snaps to your friends, landscapes of enviable places abroad? That's how Ken presented me to his friends. I was his trophy, something he had a right to own as a result of his success and personal charisma.

He never asked me about Cliff and this irritated me a little. Why wouldn't he be curious to know about my previous boyfriend? I admit I used to goad him about it sometimes when we were on the way somewhere.

'Look, Viv, I don't give a shit who you chucked to get in with me. Why should I be jealous about Keith?'

'Cliff, his name was Cliff and you know damn well it was.'

'Okay, Cliff. Why did you chuck him? I suppose it was because you met me?'

'No, actually it wasn't. I didn't know you when I finished with Cliff and the reason I chucked him is my business.'

By now Ken was frowning and his hands were gripping the steering wheel. 'Fine. In that case don't keep on mentioning him.'

I couldn't resist one more dig. I looked down into the footwell and murmured, 'Don't you even want to know whether Cliff and I did it?'

'No, I'm not remotely interested.'

And he wasn't, the bastard.

Being a trophy, though, that's supposed to be awful for the girl herself, except that it quite appealed to me. At parties, Ken would drawl, 'This is my girlfriend, Viv.' Then he'd pause to wait for a reaction from his rapt audience. I don't know quite what he expected but I would just simper with one hand on my hip, trying to be Diana Rigg.

One comment which did upset him, though, was, 'She looks a lot younger than you, Choker.'

That was at a twenty-first in Stonnall. He hates being called Choker at parties as well. I revelled in all the attention. Sometimes I'd get, 'So you're going to university, Viv?' from someone.

'That's right,' I'd smirk into my Martini Rosso, 'to read English Literature.'

Ken loved that, because it reflected glory on him, having an intellectual girlfriend to undress in his car.

Anyway, I can see a bedraggled figure struggling towards the car with a jerry can. He said he'd get two gallons at the most, otherwise it would be impossible to carry. He doesn't look very happy but I've done a packed lunch to eat at the top of Barr Beacon, so that should cheer him up a bit. I've put twice as much food for him, because he eats so fast that his hands become a blur as he stuffs his food into his mouth. That's one aspect of Ken which isn't smooth. Also, I need to have a serious chat with him, because all may not be well with me at the moment.

* * *

44

'Hello, Viv? I'm ever so glad you phoned me. I wanted to say how sorry I was to hear about Kenneth. I didn't go to the funeral, because I didn't know him that well and my brother doesn't like the Whale family, although he's always fancied you. What a horrible way to die, Viv, choking to death. I know they called him Choker but that was a dreadful thing to happen, and him in his early twenties.'

'Yes, he died right next to me. It was weird, Fran, interesting in an odd sort of way.'

'Interesting? That sounds a bit ghoulish, Viv. What did you do to help him? I heard you were sitting next to him in his car.'

'Yes, I was. I just sat and watched. I sat and watched him choke to death. He kept grabbing hold of me but I just unhooked his fingers. He tried to say things as he faded away but I took no notice. I always wondered what someone would look like when they were choking to death.'

'Jesus, Viv! You really are awful. I'm your best friend and even I'm disgusted. I heard you were hysterical when some people stopped to try to help.'

'True. My dad always said I was a drama queen.'

'Viv, I'm not sure I want to talk to you any longer. Anyway your money will run out soon.'

'Okay, I'm off now. Do thank your brother for the money and tell him yes, I will go out with him.'

'Money? What money? I didn't know Harvey had given you any money. I hope it wasn't his twenty-first money. He'd give it all to you if you flashed your eyes at him. What's it for?'

'Well, as you don't want to talk to me or to be my friend, I can't tell you. Goodbye.'

* * *

9, Brudenell Avenue,
Leeds 6,
W. Yorks.

3rd October 1965

Dear Viv,

Wonderful to hear from you! I'm so pleased you've decided to come to Leeds University and of course you can stay at my flat until you get sorted out. I've even got tickets for a Zoot Money concert in Dewsbury on your first weekend here.

I was desperately sorry to hear about the tragic death of your boyfriend, which even appeared in the *Walsall Observer* that my father sent me. Thank you for being so frank with me about the other matter. You know my feelings for you and if you decide to stay with me, I don't mind a third person appearing in our midst. Freshers' Week starts very soon and I will come down to the City Station and meet you when you get in from New Street. I shall spoil you and treat you as if you were made of porcelain.

Yours, in great anticipation,

Cliff

* * *

'Look, I told you I'd get the money and I will. Don't start getting grumpy and being Alf Garnett.'

'I gave you that money to help you on your way when you start at Leeds. It was for books, rent and fees. You must have received your cheque by now from the grant people.'

'Oh Harvey, I'm really so sorry, the cheque has gone to Leeds, to the flat where I'll be staying. Once I get up there, I'll send you a cheque in the post.'

'For Christ's sake, Viv! I lent you a hundred quid, my twenty-first birthday money. If any of my family finds out what I've done with it, I'll get kicked out. I hope you haven't discussed this with my sister.'

'Of course not, Harvey, relax. Don't you trust me?'

'I'm not sure I do any more. Even my sister's not sure about you these days.'

'I know how to restore your trust, Harvo. Just put your hand here, go on, just here, that's right.'

'Viv, I'm not sure I should be doing this here in public.'

'No one's looking, Harvo. I know you're worried about the money, so I'll do you another favour – if you still want me, that is. Oh yes, I can tell that you do.'

* * *

121, Redhouse Avenue,
Aldridge,
Staffs.

8th October 1965

Dear Cliff,

You are so kind to put me up at your flat and so understanding about my situation. What a way to start my first year at Leeds! Still, we might become one big happy family, don't you think so, Cliff? Inside this envelope I've put my arrival details on a little card. I hope you like this little touch. I could do so many little things for you, Cliff. I'm certain I could make you really happy. I'm so looking forward to us being together very soon.

Love,

Viv

PS I hate to bother you with this but could you lend me a hundred pounds? I spent so much on books for my course and naturally there are my fees to pay. I know it seems quite a lot of money but please try to do it for me. I'll make you glad you did.

ALASTAIR'S TRIUMPH

Who are you?
(The Who)

No one would blame you for looking twice at the unlikely couple walking in Sutton Park in the summer of 1969. Most young couples look more or less evenly matched. Sometimes one person may be a little more attractive than the other or a little taller, a little more vivacious or a little better dressed. But the two young people strolling under the bright oak foliage were very different. The young woman, in her early twenties, was strikingly pretty, with her short dark hair and laughing mouth. Her head was thrown back, her arms were wide and she was clearly at ease, her laughter ringing round the old trees. Beside her, smiling diffidently, the young man trampled over the uneven grass, troubled by flies but as happy as he was capable of being. Because he was very aware of his companion's presence, he tended to look down and avoid eye contact with her. She, in contrast, looked at him every few seconds and playfully goaded him for responses and reactions. The dappled shadows slid over their heads and down their backs, as they walked on towards the 1970s.

Although Alastair Humphreys was the same age as his attractive companion, he gave an impression of much more seriousness of mind and he trod warily as if he expected to stray into a minefield. Daphne, on the other hand, skipped along, as if her girlhood was still with her and every step was a new discovery.

Nor would anyone blame you for wondering how these two people came to be together. Alastair's bashfulness could not hide his adoration of this captivating young woman. She, in turn, adored his company, even if not his person, though it was easy to believe that his person might be included at some later date.

Four Beeches Comprehensive School had not been a comfortable place for Alastair. In his first year as a Biology teacher, he frequently felt like running out of the staff room. He was a square peg. He did not drink beer, he did not watch football or cricket, he had never been drunk in his life and he did not make lewd remarks to the ladies. The other male teachers would sit in a cluster in the old staff-room armchairs, their legs draped over the sides, and talk and laugh so loudly that all other conversation was drowned out. The other probationary teachers had quickly found their feet in the staff-room freemasonry and seemed casual and at ease among their senior colleagues. They would make high-pitched noises, whistles and clicks when a lady member of staff bent over a low coffee table and would go positively amok when the lovely Miss Daphne Lionel made an appearance, lighting up the dowdy room, the overloaded cork notice boards, the puddled coffee tables, the paper-strewn window sill.

Daphne, a schoolteacher version of Natalie Wood, was the object of most of the men's fancies. Neither did the sixth-form boys fail to follow her swaying hips with their eyes, as she made her way down the Marley-tiled corridors. She was a lively and popular young English teacher, surrounded by pupils during break time and by colleagues in the staff room.

So how did that most unlikely of men, Alastair Humphreys, come to be in her company? This was a man that some senior pupils snorted at in contempt, that staff watched out of the corner of their eye and then smirked about to each other. He could never find a chair to sit on in the staff room, his name was on no rotas or lists for table tennis or the weekly general knowledge quiz. He would stand awkwardly, endlessly stirring his mug of tea and searching the sea of heads for someone to chat to.

At home, however, in his narrow flat, he could be a special agent, an airline pilot or a wealthy ladies' man. Here, he never pushed a door that said 'pull' on it and he knew exactly what to say on every occasion. Ladies admired him and secretly lusted after his body. He would casually flip open his wallet and extract bank notes with easy generosity. Whether the television were on or off, the fantasy continued. It only came to an end when he walked into his first lesson the following morning to adolescent jeers – 'Hum-phreys, Hum-phreys, Hum-phreys!' The suave special agent mumbled his way through the dull lesson, regularly punctuating his monologue with 'Quiet please! Quiet please!'

Alastair's John Lennon sideburns had never quite worked either. They were thin and unconvincing and he had considered dyeing them to give them more definition. His little round glasses were genuine, because he was short-sighted, but practically they did little for his peripheral vision. Every teacher knows the importance of peripheral vision. If one of his girl pupils asked to go to the toilet, he would flush with embarrassment and search in vain for the smooth-talking ladies' man.

Alastair drove an old Triumph Spitfire, an early Sixties model in powder blue. It consisted of as much body-filler as steel and its engine sounded like a cement mixer. But it was a sports car, part of the trappings of life in the fast lane and, from a distance, Alastair was completely convinced that he was John Lennon's double, despite thumping over the potholes, the ill-fitting doors rattling.

Alastair's imitation leather flying jacket did not make a leathery noise at all, rather the sound of a plastic cloth being spread over a picnic table. His white cheesecloth shirt served only to emphasise his skinny frame. His denim jeans were somehow too new-looking and he would insist on having a crease in the legs. Sometimes, in order to look really casual, he would go out in white plimsolls. He was sure he'd seen the Beatles dressed this way in some picture or other; at least, he was certain John Lennon had worn them, or if he hadn't, he definitely would. The truth was that, even if John Lennon had worn them, he would not have resembled a redundant PE teacher clad from the local charity shop.

The Wednesday evening after the staff meeting was warm and sunny and a gentle breeze stirred the litter in little eddies.

A quiet sleepiness hung over the eerily silent buildings of Four Beeches Comprehensive. The staff car park lay in the sun on the west side, the warm tarmac turning slowly soft, as a scattering of half-hearted crows scavenged for scraps the children had left behind. The ugly modern architecture cast angular shadows and the sunlight flashed painfully from the many windows. In those days lots of glass was very trendy. No one had foreseen that this would produce classrooms like a forerunner of the microwave in summer and a simulation of the Arctic in winter.

The teachers filed out of the swing door, not pausing for conversation with each other. It had been a long, hot day, the pupils had been moody and sleepy and, at after five o'clock in the evening, their tormentors wanted to get home. One by one the cars crawled up the drive and out of the gate: a Triumph Herald, a Morris Minor, an Austin A40, a Mini Clubman. Little by little the car park emptied.

Just as the silence was almost complete, the retching of a dying starter motor echoed round the hot walls. There was a silence. Then the noise of the starter motor again. Then another silence. Daphne Lionel's little hand slapped against the steering wheel.

'Damn, damn, damn! That's all I need.' Daphne scanned around the car park, toying with her love beads. Only one vehicle remained sitting in the heat, a battered old Triumph Spitfire and, inside it, about to fire it up, was Alastair Humphreys. Daphne threw her door open and ran towards the Spitfire, tugging her miniskirt down as she went, which gave her a strange crouching gait, as if she were about to ambush Mr Humphreys.

'Mr Humphreys, do you know anything about cars?'

Alastair squinted up at her, quite taken aback by this apparition of loveliness. Sitting in his Spitfire, his eyes were just about level with the hem of Miss Lionel's skirt. Banishing some quite unacceptable fantasies from his mind, he prepared to speak to her in as deep a voice as possible. 'Miss Lionel, what seems to be the trouble?'

'My car won't start and the battery's going flat. I don't suppose you have any jump leads?'

Alastair's heart sank. What sort of a smoothie was he without even a pair of jump leads? It only worked in his imagination, whereas this was real.

For a moment he was flummoxed, but he knew he had to be masterful, cool and confident.

'Why don't you lock it up and leave it here and I'll take you home. I don't have any jump leads but I'll buy a pair on the way and I'll call for you in the morning and drive you to work.'

There! That sounded quite good. Alastair was pleased with that. He walked with her, as she went to retrieve her handbag and lock her car. He was gratified to note that he was much taller than her and drew in his breath to make himself even taller.

'Thank you so much, Mr Humphreys.'

'Please call me Alastair.' Then he cursed himself, suddenly aware that Al might sound better. No one had ever called him Al in his life but it sounded quite American, like a man who carried a gun and smoked cigars.

'Daphne.'

Alastair realised he had one evening in which to learn how to use jump leads. This had to be done. Tomorrow morning there would be colleagues milling around the car park and even pupils. He could not afford to look like a nincompoop, thrashing about amid a shower of sparks and being electrocuted in front of Daphne Lionel.

Alastair's success in starting Daphne's ailing little Riley Elf did more than inject life into its battery, it also kick-started a friendship between Daphne and Alastair. The following weekend found them sitting outside a café on Cannock Chase. The clouds were low and threatened rain. The pines stood dark and quiet and the wind was chilly.

'This is nice, Alastair. Tell me something,' she leaned forward across the wooden table, 'do I make you nervous?'

'Well, yes, not you personally, just everything. I'm a more severe version of that teacher on TV in *Please Sir!*' He glanced at her, then looked away.

'If you were that nervous,' Daphne continued, looking at his lowered face, 'you wouldn't be here now, with me.'

'I'm grateful you came.'

She laughed quietly. 'You don't have to be grateful. I came because I wanted to spend this afternoon with you.' She sipped her coffee, then turned up the collar of her coat. She went on, 'And you're treating me. Your car and your drinks.'

'I might as well spend what's left after Roy Jenkins has finished taxing me!' Alastair was pleased to see Daphne laughing at his comment. Alastair laughed with her and then, becoming suddenly serious, asked, 'Daphne, come on, what is a beautiful girl like you doing wasting time with a bumbling idiot like me?'

'I knew you were thinking something like that. You have such a low opinion of yourself, Alastair.'

'It's only the same opinion that other people have of me.' He raised his eyebrows and lifted his upturned hands in a gesture of helplessness.

'Chicken and egg, Alastair.'

'What? That's quite Monty Pythonesque.'

'People tend to see you as you see yourself.'

Alastair smiled and leaned back in his chair, waving his teaspoon as if conducting an orchestra. 'No, no, Daphne, I can't go for that! However anybody looks at you, you are very beautiful.' He knew he was blushing but he didn't care, and the cold wind kept his rising colour in check.

'You are very sweet, Alastair, but it's not just a question of looks. Whatever you may look like, if you are a total shit, everything about you will show it and people will see it.'

'The kids don't like me, nor do the staff.'

'That's because you don't like yourself.'

'And what the hell am I supposed to do about that?'

Daphne now leaned right forward into his face, forcing him to look at her. She said, 'First, you have to find out who you are.'

This was a revolutionary idea to Alastair, something he had never considered. He had always assumed you just live your life, people come and go and things happen to you, some good and some bad. It seemed to him that people liking you or not liking you came from them, not from yourself. Daphne was saying that people's reaction to you was somehow determined not by who they are but by who or what you are yourself.

Her eyes were still on him. He made an effort to look up at her: 'When I went to grammar school in 1958 I was freckled, skinny and short-sighted. I had no friends and girls laughed at me. Now I'm nearly twenty-three and just a bigger version of that schoolboy.' He sat back, exhausted. He'd never been so open with anyone before. He should be terrified of Daphne, yet he felt quite at ease with her.

She smiled at him over her coffee cup. 'Men all think the same way. They believe you have to be a six-foot muscle-man with looks like Steve McQueen in order to be attractive or popular. It really is bunk.'

Alastair felt a few spots of rain and was aware of the clatter of crockery and cutlery coming from the open serving hatch of the café. They weren't doing much business. He was glad about that, although he appreciated it was not such good news for the proprietors.

'So what do I do now to improve myself and to become a proper person, a fully fledged member of the human race?'

She was appraising him now and chose her words with care: 'Number one, get rid of those sideburns, they really are not you. Number two, don't worry about John Lennon. Alastair, you don't look like John Lennon and you don't need to. You are an individual, bookish and eccentric, and these are the things that people will accept are a part of you. If you have enough faith in yourself, other men will actually envy you and try to copy you.'

Alastair sat in thought for a long time, slowly stirring his lukewarm coffee, as pieces of a jigsaw puzzle swam around in his head and gradually began to fit together.

Alastair sat alone in his flat. In front of him on the circular white table was a rectangular mirror which he used for shaving. It was propped up against a pile of books and he drew up his chair, a man about to talk to his own reflection. Outside in the darkness a heavy rain drummed against the windows but the curtains were open and the noise of the rain somehow increased the feeling of cosiness and security in the room. Alastair rubbed his hands together and braced himself, like a man about to dive into cold water. This was almost a mystical ceremony. This was the finding of Alastair Humphreys.

First, he recited his name over and over again into the mirror. Then, when he reached a heightened state of awareness of himself, he started asking, 'Who are you?' He did this for several minutes as the rain beat down outside.

Alastair began to see himself as if from a distance of several feet. He was one of many, not a person stuck inside his own body, unable to get out. He could be one of a crowd with all his own special qualities, he was no better and no worse. He would no longer be a laughable imitation of somebody different, but a man, secure and comfortable as the person he actually was. He told himself that if someone laughed at him, it would be in an affectionate rather than a spiteful way. He would respond by smiling, being relaxed and accepting the fact that he was an individual and that he was being recognised as such.

Later that evening he shaved off his sideburns and determined to have his hair cut into a proper style. He would also update his wardrobe. Away would go the latter-day student and in would come the more modern young man who was ready to mix with others as an equal. Using his reflection in the long black window, he practised standing tall with his head up, so that he could make eye contact with others. He would get into the habit of holding his head up and of squaring his shoulders. Why had he stooped anyway? Why had he withdrawn into himself, ready to curl up like a wounded animal? He would make the most of his height and develop a physical presence. He would modulate his voice instead of whispering, and would be convinced of the worth of what he had to say. Monday would be his launch date. He would be taking off before the moon expedition. He was several days ahead of Neil Armstrong.

By November both Neil Armstrong and Alastair Humphreys had completed their mission. A dank, grey mist hung about Four Beeches Comprehensive School. There was no wind and because of the murk, you could hardly see across the playground to the Science block. Everything was dripping wet and the damp was of that special quality that penetrates any clothing and even gets into your skin and bones.

Break came at eleven o'clock. Hand bells were rung all over the building, chairs scraped and cascades of footsteps washed through the corridors and down flights of stairs. An unruly queue formed at the tuck shop in the dining room, while a game of football that was, in reality, more like a fight, broke out in the cold, raw playground. The boys appeared quite impervious to the cold and damp.

The staff room was on the ground floor and opened onto a busy corridor. Outside the door stood a noisy but good-humoured bunch of second-year pupils. There was a hushed argument, which ended when one of them was chosen to knock on the staff-room door. The door swung open and out wafted a cloud of tobacco smoke. Through the blue haze, Mr Banks appeared in his academic gown like Count Dracula. Mr Banks peered balefully down at the children, adjusting his spectacles as if he could not quite believe the horrible sight before him. Mr Banks was one of those old-style schoolmasters who believe strongly in education but disapprove heartily of its little consumers.

'Well?' he intoned. 'Don't tell me, you wish to speak to Mr Humphreys. Everyone wishes to speak to Mr Humphreys. The whole world seems to wish to speak to Mr Humphreys. Can the poor man not enjoy his break unmolested?'

'Yes sir, I mean no sir, I mean is Mr Humphreys there, sir?'

'What business is it of yours, any of you,' his bleary eyes swept across the huddle of faces, 'where Mr Humphreys may or may not be at this or any time?'

'We've come to talk to him, sir,' piped a little voice.

'We like talking to Mr Humphreys,' came another voice.

Mr Banks continued to study the pupils before him as if they were some kind of infection: 'Very gratifying, I'm sure.' He turned towards the smoke and noise of cups and saucers. 'I will go and dislodge Mr Humphreys for you. Wait there.' The children were almost jumping up and down with excitement.

The end of term came ever nearer and the long summer holiday lay just over the horizon. The curriculum at Four Beeches gradually degenerated into quizzes, plays and other activities. Pupils would be seen pattering along corridors with full make-up, dressed as elves or paupers from Dickens. Rehearsals disrupted all attempts at proper lessons and a sort of carnival atmosphere reigned. Alastair Humphreys decided that if this was the dawning of the Age of Aquarius, it would do quite nicely thank you – no lesson preparation, no books to mark.

It was the end of school on Thursday afternoon and steady rain had been falling for hours. Alastair left the building and trotted towards his new Mini. This was not quite like his previous rakish image but then, who needed it? Alastair didn't. Trotting behind him were a boy and a girl, splashing through the puddles, one carrying his briefcase, the other a sheaf of papers.

Parked next to Alastair was the headmaster's Rover, and indeed Mr Sims himself was stooping to take things out of the boot. He rose stiffly and peered at Alastair, a good-humoured smile creasing his face: 'Ah, Mr Humphreys and his faithful retinue! They come out to carry your burden in all weathers. Very good, very good.' Mr Sims closed his boot and staggered away with his cardboard box. As he disappeared towards the building, he could still be heard muttering, 'Yes, very good, Mr Humphreys, keep it up, keep it up.'

Alastair and his two helpers looked at each other and giggled about Mr Sims, the rain pattering on their hair. Alastair took his key and bent to unlock his car door. He thanked his helpers and told them they could go. He felt the cold rain trickling down his neck and wished he had brought a raincoat. Still, within a quarter of an hour he would be at Daphne Lionel's flat, having his regular cup of tea and chat about the day.

'Alastair! Alastair! Don't go yet, hold on a minute.' Leaning on the open door, Alastair turned to behold Jim Turret, PE teacher and sex symbol.

Tall and fit-looking, with a tanned face and a mop of dark hair, Jim looked like a male model. He spoke with a very loud voice and was always laughing and slapping other men on the shoulder. He had many female admirers on the staff and among the senior girls. Nevertheless, although Jim fancied Miss Lionel enormously, it was Alastair and not he who would be taking tea with her and who was obviously quite close to her. This baffled Jim and he wondered bitterly whether Alastair was shagging her. He hoped not, for this reduced his own 'market'. At the beginning of the school year in September he had regarded Alastair with amused contempt. The man was a joke. He looked ridiculous and his every move was awkward and clumsy. Nowadays Jim was not so sure. Alastair too had lady admirers and was popular with the pupils. A mystifying change had come over him, so that Jim now felt he needed to count him among the privileged circle of his friends.

'Alastair, we're doing circuit training in the gym when all the kids have gone,' Jim said, puffing out his chest and pulling his shoulders back, 'why don't you come and join us?'

Jim stretched himself and was disappointed to notice that he did not tower above Alastair. In fact Alastair, who used to stoop and slouch, now stood much taller. Jim rested a hand on the roof of Alastair's Mini, so that their height difference didn't matter anyway, and waited for Alastair to make an embarrassed and uncomfortable response to his invitation.

To Jim's dismay, Alastair threw his head back and laughed into the rain. It was a warm-hearted and easy laugh. Jim started with surprise as Alastair patted him on the upper arm and said, 'Thanks, Jim, but I'm off to Daphne Lionel's. In any case circuit training would kill me off and everyone knows how I hate exertion of almost any kind!' Only then did Alastair release Jim's arm and take his eyes from his face. Jim was not sure why but he felt as if he had somehow lost points.

'Fine, that's okay. Well, see you around.' Jim sauntered off with his head down and his hands in his pockets.

A few minutes' drive away in a leafy suburb of north Birmingham stood two small residential blocks. Surrounded by mature silver birch and beech trees, they were only two storeys high and the generous windows had colourful window boxes. Alastair pulled into the tidy little car park with its white markings and left the Mini under the trees. Still the rain pattered down, puddling the tarmac and making rustling noises in the rich greenery.

Daphne lived on the first floor. When she opened the door to Alastair, she was wearing jeans and a kaftan and he could smell the tea brewing. The airy lounge was fresh, Daphne had opened all the windows, though from another room came a faint aroma of joss sticks.

'Guess what I've bought for you.' Alastair looked at her, waiting. 'Ginger nuts.'

Alastair beamed. 'The way to a man's heart.' He sat on the narrow settee and looked at her expectantly.

She looked back at him, as she poured the tea. 'What?'

Alastair replied, 'Something's wrong. You want to talk about something.'

Daphne bent to hand him his mug. Her love beads fell forward. 'Amazing. Am I so obvious?'

Alastair sipped his tea. 'You're not obvious at all, Daphne. It's just that we know each other well enough. I noticed your face in assembly this morning. You didn't join in the hymn.'

'I'm not that keen on "To be a Pilgrim".'

'I noticed you at lunchtime too. Your mind was somewhere else. I waved to you but you didn't notice.'

'Sorry.' She sat beside him and nursed her tea thoughtfully in her lap. Alastair drank and waited. He was good at waiting. He used to spend much of his life waiting.

At length Daphne began, 'I'm going to leave teaching.'

Alastair stared at her, 'You mean you're going to leave Four Beeches?'

'No, Alastair, I mean I'm going to leave teaching, the profession, the vocation, the job, call it whatever you like.'

'But you're so good at it.'

Daphne turned towards him. 'No, I'm not, Alastair. I'm popular and the kids like me because I'm young and look okay but I have no control in class and the kids don't respect me, not in the way they respect you, and they learn from you as well.'

Alastair thought about this for a moment. He had always admired Daphne so much and he found it difficult to accept that she had flaws.

'What will you do?' he asked.

'That is what I wanted to ask you about.'

Alastair's eyes opened wide in astonishment. He put his mug down on the low coffee table and turned to her: 'Me? How can I help? Remember, Daphne, I was a complete mess until I met you. It was you who put my life in order. I'm sorry to say that doesn't mean I can do the same for you.'

Daphne smiled at him weakly and took his hand in hers: 'Yes, you can. Only you can do this for me. It's your turn now to help me. Who am I, Alastair?'

Alastair sat back against the settee, looking up at the ceiling. Here was a very new challenge for him! Daphne was his best friend and his role now was to mentor her as she had him.

'Shouldn't you be looking into a mirror?' asked Alastair, feeling rather uncertain.

'Not necessarily. Really I suppose I already know *who* I am but I'm not sure *what* I am. It's more of a professional question. What would I be good at?'

Alastair smiled, 'That's easy. You're a very good listener and you have an instinctive understanding of what makes people tick. You could do another degree and become a psycho-analyst. You would be really good.'

The last day of term is always chaos. Alastair had looked out for Daphne during the morning, as he had traipsed from one informal quiz lesson to the next. The usual rule of keeping to the left of the corridor had collapsed into anarchy and pupils seemed to be milling around as they pleased. Because it was a hot morning, the standard of uniform was not good either. There were open-neck shirts and missing blazers. So it was at the beginning of morning break that Alastair at last beheld Daphne among a sea of children going downstairs in front of him. In the crush of bodies Alastair struggled even to raise his hand from his side, so instead of waving, he called out, 'Miss Lionel, Miss Lionel!'

Daphne turned and smiled. She looked less tired than of late. Alastair thought her face looked alive again, just as it had used to. They stood back against the wall as droves of children pushed past. Before he could speak, she said, raising her voice above the din, 'Thank you, Alastair. You are a true friend. I won't kiss you on the cheek in front of the kids. You'll just have to imagine it.'

'Oh, I frequently do,' he laughed and she joined in. Then he added, 'But what have I done to deserve my imaginary kiss?'

'You've sorted me out. I've given it lots of thought and I'm not cut out for teaching. I'm going back to university to study psychology and I want to train to be a therapist.'

Alastair looked down at her, quite unaware of the hubbub around him and said to her, 'I'm going to miss you.'

'You won't get a chance. I'm going to Birmingham University and you'll be coming to visit me every week.'

Alastair grinned. Life was good.

Raymond wasn't bored. He was never bored, it was just that sometimes he couldn't find anything to do.

He was quite a solitary boy. He had a few friends from school that he would sit on a wall and smoke with. They would spit on the ground and say very little. When he had some money he would go into Leslie's the newsagent and buy a Jamboree Bag or a liquorice stick. Sometimes he would cycle down the high street with his arms crossed, hoping that people on the kerbside would admire his skill.

He had bright ginger hair like the Thermogene they used to put on your chest, and freckles, especially on his nose. He had a harelip, the result of an accident when he was a child. That same accident caused him to walk bandy-legged, turning his right foot out as he went along.

Raymond would have been quite good at school but his mind was always elsewhere. Sitting in the classroom, his green eyes would be fixed on the towering clouds in the windy sky outside the window. His mind would be in the deep, sandy quarry where the boys used to spin saucepan lids ferretted out from the fly-tipped rubbish, like Frisbees. What Raymond lacked was direction, something which his easygoing parents, unusually easygoing for 1962, had failed to give him. He called his father Pete, something greatly envied by boys who knew him, and he referred to his mother as 'the old gel', giving him that allure of a boy old before his time.

But there was something missing in Raymond's life, even though he couldn't have told you what it was. He loved to stand on the railway bridge, lean over the wall and let the acrid smoke billow over him and blot out the world. He liked to squat in the lane outside his house and play marbles all on his own, watching the bright colours rotate inside the glass balls and holding them up to his eye to see a different world inside. He liked to let sherbet dissolve on his tongue and he liked it when he sat too close to the kitchen stove, so that his face glowed red and hot and he would run upstairs to the little bathroom and look at himself in his dad's round shaving mirror. But none of these things was a direction at all, just part of a thirteen-year-old's day. If you asked Raymond what his life was really about, he would pull a funny face and tug at one of his ears, then tell you he wanted to be an engine driver or Marty Wilde.

Be all that as it may, Raymond was quite insecure. You couldn't tell. He always wore a bit of a grin, his tie askew and at least part of his grey flannel shirt hanging out under his woolly jumper. Several things made Raymond feel insecure. He used to have a funny notion as he walked and skipped home from school that his house would be empty and that the rest of the family had gone away for ever and left him all alone. He used to worry that he would get ill and die before he had lived long enough to have a real girlfriend. He feared he would wake up one morning and have no voice and never be able to speak again. He wondered whether his voice would never break or whether he would have to have false teeth when he grew up. His friend Harvey once told him in a whisper that, if you were constipated for more than three days, your stomach would burst and its contents splatter all round the room. Consequently, if Raymond missed a day or two in the toilet, the grin would be noticeably absent from his freckly face.

He rarely got told off. This was probably because he spent so much time out of doors. He would scamper over the fields with Bruce, a black and white mongrel that belonged to one of the neighbours. Raymond felt that Bruce was his dog, although he never obeyed him and once peed on his shoes. Raymond and Bruce would sit on Churn Hill, the wind blowing their eyes into slits, and look at nothing, content in each other's company. Raymond would reach out and put his arm round Bruce's barrel-like body and Bruce would respond by licking Raymond's face. Bruce's breath was terrible but Raymond's mother had told him that his was too.

The November afternoon was so dark that the lights were on in the classroom. This gave a feeling of early festivity, as if Christmas were just around the corner. It was the early darkness, the bitter cold and the idea of anticipation of something, which only children can experience fully. Mr London droned on about crotchets, minims and quavers. He used a wooden recorder as a pointer, waving it in front of the class to beat time and tapping with it on the blackboard to point at the musical notation. In front of each pupil on the desk lid lay the recorder that was shortly to be picked up and played. Raymond could smell the Dettol on the mouthpiece and quite liked the taste. He wondered idly what it would be like to drink Dettol and decided it would be like Tizer, because the colours were not that different. But could you disinfect a recorder with Tizer?

'Kennedy, are you with us?' Mr London's raised eyebrows caused big creases in his forehead like that breed of dog, Raymond thought, the one that has a barrel of brandy round its neck.

'Yes sir.' Raymond's real nightmare at this juncture was that Mr London would invite him to the front of the class with his recorder to give a rendition of 'Nymphs and Shepherds'.

'Then please try to do me the courtesy of feigning vague interest, just to make me feel I have a role to play in this school.'

Raymond wasn't sure what feigning meant but he recognised sarcasm when he heard it. He started counting inside his head and aimed at getting to five hundred as a way to pass the time. It worked. The bell monitor tolled out the end of the music lesson and noises were heard on the stairs outside. Mr London was 3G's form teacher and told them all that he wanted to speak to them before they went to the last lesson of the day. Raymond had stopped counting. This might be interesting. A special announcement often meant that someone was going to get punished, or better still, a boy might get caned.

'At registration tomorrow we shall have a new boy here. His name is Sean Quinn and he is a traveller.' Thirty-two puzzled faces turned towards Mr London. 'To you people that means a gypsy. He may not stay with us long but while he is with us

I have assigned a boy to show him the ropes and to act as his friend and mentor. That boy is Raymond Kennedy.'

Raymond had been lost in thought about brightly coloured wagons drawn by shire horses and old hags gazing at crystal balls. He also wondered what a mentor was. It sounded like a kind of boiled sweet.

'When you are fully awake, Kennedy, I'd like to ask you to come and see me after school for a short while. I know you don't catch the bus, because I have observed you dicing with death on your bicycle.'

Raymond wondered why Mr London had chosen him for this responsible job. Perhaps he saw in Raymond hidden qualities that others felt were not there at all. Or perhaps he thought Raymond was so immature that a job like this might make him grow up a little. Even at thirteen Raymond had lived long enough to know that the unpalatable alternative was usually the correct one.

The two boys wandered over the narrow patch of wild ground known as the Spinney and on up to Churn Hill. It was bitterly cold and their cheeks were red. Running through long grass, nettles and bushes had soaked their jeans and shoes, because the early frost had turned to water. Their shining faces were surrounded by clouds of steam and each panted breath added to it.

Sean was smaller than Raymond, with wiry blond hair that stood up like a brush and steely grey eyes that were almost abnormally wide open. All this gave him an expression of permanent astonishment. His skin had that outdoor shade – was it tanned, tawny or just dirty? He stood loose-limbed and alert, as if ready to take to his heels at any moment.

Under a craggy oak tree, its black fingers reaching to the colourless sky, they stopped, bent forward with their hands on their knees and tried to catch their breath.

'Why don't you live in a house like me?' Raymond turned to his friend, pulled a face and tugged his ear.

'Because people are meant to wander. My da says all the trouble started with the human race when men and women stopped travelling and settled down. He says it goes back to the Ice Age. My da says that's when colds and flu started too. My da knows a lot of things.'

Sean grinned, produced a cigarette paper from his bulging trouser pocket and proceeded to roll himself a cigarette. Raymond's cheeks were turning blue and he thrust his hands under his armpits and jumped up and down.

'That won't get you warm, matey. The secret is to relax when you're cold and not to tense up. If you go slack and give in to it, you won't feel it. People in houses fight against everything and that's why they're always unhappy and get bad.' Sean drew on his cigarette with its trumpet end from which red-hot shreds of tobacco fell like stars.

Raymond wondered whether Sean would offer him a puff but he didn't. He tried to get some of the mud off the hem of his jeans and wiped his shoes on the wet grass, the way you do when you've trodden in dog's or cow's mess.

Sean laughed at him, 'There you go again, fighting against everything. You people are funny.'

'Oh,' began Raymond sarcastically, 'so you just let everything happen to you, the wet, the cold and the mud. You don't bother. My old gel will slap my head. Maybe yours won't. Can I have a drag on that?' he added peevishly, looking at his friend as if he'd just punched him. The cigarette, now barely recognisable as such, was thrust in Raymond's direction, brown with nicotine and pinched almost flat.

'Ray, matey, I'm talking about a way of looking at life, just a way that's all. I can't explain about the mud or about wet jeans. It's just a way, that's all.'

Suddenly Sean stopped talking and raised his head as if listening intently. He narrowed his steely eyes, cocked an ear and flared his nostrils, trying to pick up a faint scent that no one else could possibly be aware of. Raymond looked at him in alarm, tugging his ear and pulling a face.

'What's up, Quinny?'

Sean raised his index finger to Raymond's lips and mimed 'Ssshhh!' Raymond stood silently. He couldn't hear anything and was about to tell Sean that he was mad, when he too heard a faint rustle. It came from a holly bush a few yards ahead of them.

Sean whispered to Raymond, 'It's a pigeon.'

'How do you know, if you can't see it?'

'Because I can smell it. It's injured and in a panic.'

'I suppose you can smell that too.'

'Yes. They smell different when they're scared.' Sean turned to Raymond and looked him in the eye: 'So do people, they smell different when they're afraid.'

Sean advanced silently and knelt just inside the holly bush. There was some flapping, then silence, as he withdrew a grey and white pigeon that looked oddly relaxed in his hands. One of its wings hung down limp, instead of being folded along its back. Sean stroked it gently and rhythmically and cooed strange noises. To Raymond it seemed that he was singing to the bird. He stood transfixed.

Sean began to stretch the wing very gently and the bird offered no resistance. Then Sean made a little flicking movement and there was a soft 'click' noise. The pigeon shuddered and then, to Raymond's amazement, it folded its wing back into position. Raymond did not know what to say to his friend. Sean was like a magician. He set the pigeon down in the grass before them and they watched it waddle away and then take flight. Sean turned to Raymond, produced another cigarette paper and muttered, 'It wasn't broken, just out of joint. It happens sometimes.'

Raymond was surprised that Sean had used a match to light the fire.

'I suppose you expected me to rub two sticks together!' laughed Sean. 'Why make life more difficult for yourself? If you have matches, you use matches.'

Considering that everything seemed to be wet, getting a fire going in the corner of a field was little short of a miracle, thought

Raymond. Sean had built a makeshift hearth and surround using stones and they now had a tolerable blaze. Raymond's jeans and shoes were drying nicely and Sean had made a kind of brush with a small bunch of twigs to get the worst of the muck off. Raymond reflected with great satisfaction that he would be going home warm and dry and relatively presentable, all thanks to Sean. The two boys sat on a heap of old fencing posts and gazed into the fire, which was beginning to make them both feel quite drowsy. It was getting dark and it looked as if there might be fog.

'How long will you be staying here, Quinny?'

Sean turned to him, the flickering light playing on his face, 'Till my da says it's time to go. Anyway, we're not really welcome on Walmer Meadow. The circus people go there but Romanies get told to piss off.'

'What do you want to be when you're grown up, Quinny?'

Sean thought for a while and poked the fire with a stick, sending a shower of sparks into the darkness. 'I'll be the same as I am now, only bigger.'

Raymond tried to comprehend this, because it seemed as though Sean had no ambition at all. 'Don't you want to *be* anything, like having a job and earning money?'

'My place in life is to be a good Romany, to move with the seasons and to learn to understand this world. I don't have much call for money but I can make money if I need it. What about you, Ray? What do you want to be?'

This flummoxed Raymond completely. This was the sort of question his teachers asked him, or Pete, his dad. 'God knows! I don't think about it.'

Sean laughed and slapped Raymond on the knee. 'Well, I think it's time you bloody started, matey! You expect to have a house of your own and money of your own. How do you think you're going to get them? You won't be a kid for ever, neither of us will. You can't even light a fire or hear half the sounds in this field. You'll be a settled man, a town man.'

To Raymond just the idea of being any sort of man was a shock. Quinny was right. He couldn't go running around the fields for ever or sit daydreaming in class. He was a teenager and it was time for him to stop being a kid. He looked at Sean. Sean smoked a cigarette like a man and he could survive with his own skills. Sean fitted into his own way of life, whereas Raymond did not fit into his. As the orange and yellow sparks flitted upwards, so a change began in Raymond. He didn't want to copy Sean but he did want to be more like him. Sean would be able to command the respect of other boys and instruct them in matters about which they knew nothing. What could he, Raymond, do?

'I shall miss you, Quinny.'

'You know, Ray, you're a loner like me. But we're opposites, because I have to learn to be able to survive alone. You have to learn how to survive with other people.'

Raymond pondered this: 'But you're like a tribe, you all live together too.'

'Yes, but we pride ourselves on being able to take care of ourselves. You've got to live among the house people. You're still a kid, Ray.' And he spat into the fire. Turning to Raymond, he added, 'I shall miss you too.'

When Mrs Kennedy pushed open the door of Raymond's bedroom, she felt her jaw drop. She blinked several times, wondering whether perhaps she was in the wrong house or Ray had been replaced by another boy. She ventured inside a step at a time, gaping all around her, as if entering Aladdin's cave. What she beheld was a scene of tidiness and almost military organisation. All the school books lay on the shelf, standing together like a rank of soldiers. Ray's bed was made, which was a shock in itself, and all his clothes were tidied away into the drawers. She stood there, hands on hips, and blew a strand of hair away from her eye. Her amazement was such that she failed to hear Raymond breezing into the room. She looked at him as if he were a stranger and stammered, 'Ray, was it you – I mean, did you – do all this?' She swept a hand around the room.

Raymond beamed, 'Yup. I can't smarten my life up with a room that looks like a dump.'

'But what brought all this about?'

'Quinny.'

'What, the gypsy boy? Why would he tell you to tidy up your bedroom?'

Raymond pulled a face and tugged at his ear diffidently. 'Quinny told me I'm still a little kid who can't do anything for himself. He said I'm not becoming a man and need to be more grown up.'

Without another word Mrs Kennedy planted a kiss on her son's forehead and went downstairs. Raymond felt that this was a good start and decided to stop referring to his mother as 'the old gel'.

Later that evening Raymond's father called him into the kitchen. He stood leaning against the sink, pulling on his cherrywood pipe. Raymond noticed a smell of beer and knew his father was not quite sober.

'Well, Ray, your mother tells me you've started to grow up a bit.' Raymond waited while his father doubled up with a coughing fit and turned to spit in the sink. His father went on, his voice now much hoarser, 'Good lad, about bloody time!'

Encouraged by his father's reaction, Raymond ventured, 'I'm going to save money too.'

His father's red eyelids lifted slightly, 'Oh yes? You haven't got no money. How can you save money you haven't got?'

'I've got a job, Pete. I've got a paper round.'

Mr Kennedy's pipe almost fell from his mouth and he had to take it out in his astonishment. 'Bloody hell! What has come over you? Whatever it is, I hope it doesn't wear off.'

Over the frozen playing field ran Raymond, leaving shoe prints in the whiteness. Over the wooden footbridge that spanned the railway and into the gulley, with its broken and uneven surface, he ran. His breath came hard and smoky and he squinted ahead towards Walmer Meadow. At last he broke through the gap in the hedge – and saw: nothing. The gypsies had gone.

Barry chased the lone piece of crispy bacon around his breakfast plate. He pronged it with his fork, brought it to his nose and sniffed it. Finally he used his knife to remove it and put it back where it had started.

'That's perfectly good smoked bacon, Barry. Nothing wrong with it at all. Goodness alone knows why you still have this funny "thing" about bacon and pork sausage. I ate your sausage, as usual.'

Barry Enoch, newly a state pensioner, frowned at his plate and muttered, 'You know why it is, Jo. Don't give me such a hard time. I've eaten the rest of it.'

By now Jo Enoch had her hands on her hips, as if about to admonish a child. She looked down at her husband's bald head and sighed, 'God, Barry! You still go on about working at that slaughterhouse. We've been married nearly forty years and you worked at Harroway's long before that. When was it? Nineteen sixty-two?'

'Aye, nineteen sixty-two it was. Harroway's Pork Butchers, Bradford Street, Walsall.'

Jo knew this story so well that she was miming the address behind her husband's back. As she whisked his plate away, she slapped his bald spot playfully and said, 'Getting on for fifty years since you worked there. It was temporary anyway, you were a student. Get over it, Barry. You're retired, you can do what you like. You can even eat bacon and pork sausage.'

But Barry had slipped down memory lane as he sat wide-eyed at the breakfast table, gazing at the window but seeing nothing. The kitchen flew away and Barry became Baz Enoch again ...

Autumn 1962. Baz reckoned his hair looked like Adam Faith's. He had a bad chest too, which made him a 'sufferer', a sort of romantic hero, like those consumptive poets you learn about, coughing their guts up in the Lake District.

Baz chased his breakfast bacon round and round his greasy plate. He knew he wasn't going to eat it but wanted to postpone any decision-making. Edna Enoch pushed her knotted head-scarf back, revealing her two front curlers, and scowled at her son who sat moodily cluttering up her little kitchen.

'Don't play with it, Barry, eat it! That's perfectly good food. There's thousands of hungry children in Africa would be glad of that bacon.' Edna nodded to emphasise her point. Then she relit a stub of Capstan and inhaled deeply.

Barry looked up at her and gave a crooked smile: 'Well then, wrap it up in a parcel and I'll take it down to the post office for them.'

Barry ducked as his mother's hand flew through the air just above his head. Unsticking the stub of cigarette from her lips, she hissed, 'Don't you give me your lip, you cheeky beggar! You may be eighteen but you're not too old to get a good box round the ears!'

Summer 1962. Baz Enoch considered himself quite a catch. At nearly eighteen, he had a BSA 250 in maroon, a leather jacket with tassels and motorcycling trousers that looked leather but were not. He had a silver crash helmet but wanted a black one. He also wanted a black handkerchief as a face mask. He could jive quite well at the Saturday night 'socials' at Leighswood School and he was confident with the girls. He should leave the commercial college with British Constitution, Book-keeping and Economics. He was tall and lanky with quite good skin and he had only one serious problem in his life – he was skint. He needed money and he needed a well-paid summer job to earn it.

His growing up had been uneventful. Nothing much happened in Walsall Wood Road. The between-the-wars terraces backed on to a small coalmine and a brickworks. Among his own sort, modest and easygoing working-class folk, Baz was quite at ease. He could josh with the older men and puff on a Park Drive. The world was a predictable place, the Saturday matinee at the 'pictures' and the Number Eight coffee bar in the town centre, where Baz swaggered among the ponytails and white ankle socks.

It was on a Wednesday night in that very coffee bar that Terry shoved a copy of the *Walsall Observer* in his face and mumbled, spitting crisps and saliva, 'Look at this, Baz, this is what we need.' Clumsily he folded the newspaper into a manageable rectangle and stabbed with his index finger at one of the small ads. Baz held the newspaper up to his face in the dim light and began to read the tiny print.

Butcher's assistants wanted!
Local pork butchers require youths for summer period.
Special clothing provided, excellent rates of pay.
Telephone WAL 3181 or visit and talk to Mr Ralphs, Harroway's, Bradford Street, Walsall.

'Blimey!' grinned Baz.

As if to underline the drama of the moment, someone fed the jukebox. Number Eight shook to a rocky version of 'Red River'. Yelling at the top of your voice was now the only means of communication.

'Blimey is the word,' Terry bawled into Baz's ear, 'I've heard we could make close to twenty a week with overtime! My dad only makes seventeen quid.'

'Mess off, Terry! Don't be daft!'

Baz left his childhood behind when he pulled into the car park at Harroway's and stopped his bike by the far wall. He killed the engine and turned off the petrol tap. Terry climbed off the pillion seat, then Baz hefted the BSA on to its stand. For a long moment they looked at each other, then at the complex of sheds and offices before them. A distinct smell hung in the air, a piggy smell, a smell of death.

It was 11 a.m. and they were due to meet Mr Ralphs for a chat and a look around the works. On the telephone Mr Ralphs had said to Baz, 'If you come at eleven, most of the noisy stuff will be over and we shall be able to hear ourselves speak.' Baz had no idea what he meant and Terry had shrugged it off.

Baz ran a comb through his hair and quickly shaped his quiff, affecting a tough-guy walk and leaving his shades on to look like Roy Orbison. Terry strutted, jerking his shoulders, and considered spitting on the ground but decided against it. Both had discussed how they would quickly become well known at Harroway's, how the girls would admire them and how the men would envy them.

Mr Ralphs was a ruddy, thickset man in his forties. Under his brown cow gown, which was open at the front, could be seen a pair of broad shoulders and a deep, muscular chest. When he shook hands with Baz and Terry, their little white hands disappeared inside his shovel-like hand with its grip like a vice. Both were a little taken aback. Also, that stench was very strong.

Mr Ralphs looked hard at both young men and said sternly, 'You both realise that this is a butcher's, don't you? We kill pigs here. When they arrive, they're alive and squealing, then we kill 'em, cut 'em up and turn 'em into sausage and sides of pork, understand?'

Baz smirked cockily: 'No problem, Mr Ralphs, we can cope with that, can't we, Tez?'

'Walkover,' sniggered Terry.

Mr Ralphs looked at them doubtfully from the corner of his eye and his expression showed he had heard it all before and he knew exactly what was coming next. He took an armful of huge plastic smocks from a hook, then checked the youths' shoe sizes and handed them a pair of boots each. Finally he gave them each an elasticated mob-cap and waited while they got kitted up. Baz and Terry were astonished at all this ritual and thought it seemed far too dramatic.

Baz turned to Mr Ralphs, 'Do we really need these boots and these hats?' He was concerned that his hair could no longer be seen and was squashed out of shape by this dreadful cap.

Mr Ralphs compressed his lips and breathed in patiently. 'Well, you don't want mess all over your clothes, face and hair, do you now?'

'Mess?' piped Terry uneasily.

'What sort of mess, Mr Ralphs?' quavered Baz, considerably less cocky than before.

Mr Ralphs threw his head back and laughed a deep laugh, slapping his muscular thighs. Then he bared his teeth at them in a fierce grin and screwed up his eyes. 'Why, *blood* of course, blood and guts!'

Baz and Terry flinched and took a step back.

Once again on day three, Terry stood patiently beside the BSA while Baz brought his breakfast up by the wall.

'You sure you want to do this, Baz? We don't have to do it, you know.'

Baz spat and blew his nose: 'It's just nerves, Tez. I've got to do it, I need the dough.'

As they stumbled over the puddled rubble of the narrow car park, Baz cast his mind back to five-thirty yesterday evening, the front of his hair black with crusted blood and his sideburns caked with it. In his nostrils there still hung the stink of butchery. It wasn't just the padded calipers, on the beasts' necks, delivering the death-shock and bringing them like a sack of spuds to the ground; it wasn't just the squealing that sounded like murdered children and drowned every other sound; it wasn't even the upside-down carcasses that splashed their life-blood all over the white-tiled killing floor. The final straw had been the acrid stink of the hair being singed off the carcasses with blowlamps. It was the whole overwhelming shock of sudden death and the sight and smell of blood, warm intestines and glistening lungs. Baz had stared, dumbstruck, as the skilled slaughterman took up his vicious-looking knife on day one. He opened up the inverted carcass from groin to throat, opened up the ribcage and, with three deft cuts, released the entire 'pluck'. This latter slid and splattered to the tiles at his feet, like a bucket of wet fish. Baz had kept pinching his nose, so as not to start heaving there and then. The slaughterman, covered in dark red slime, had turned to him angrily and yelled, 'Oi! You there, nancy boy, are you helping me or puking on your boots? You useless little arse-wipe!'

'Sorry, sir,' whimpered Baz, his mouth full of saliva, swallowing convulsively.

The walk to the motorbike at the end of work was now a quieter affair. There was no swaggering. Baz and Tez walked quietly across the rubble, talking softly and scratching their heads wearily, just like all the other men. The boyishness was being knocked out of them. They put their helmets on and looked at each other grimly. Tez said, 'Just think, Baz, we look just like those pigs inside our bodies.'

Baz glanced at him, chewing the nail on his little finger, 'How do you mean?'

'Well, think about it, we're really just lots of blood and fat and bags of stuff.'

'And a brain, don't forget the brain. Ours is bigger than a pig's.'

Tez elbowed him in the ribs and laughed, 'Yours isn't, mate! Yours is probably smaller!'

Baz was still serious: 'Think about it, Tez, we've both seen loads of brains in the last few days. It's just grey jelly.'

He was staring wide-eyed at Tez, who replied, 'I know, I've had it all over the soles of my boots. What's your point?'

'Well, if we've seen all the lungs, heart and everything and we've seen the brain,' here he paused to jerk the BSA off its stand, 'where's the soul?'

'What?'

'Where's the soul, Tez?'

Number Eight on a Thursday evening is usually packed. This was a summer's night and the glass door was wedged open, so you could see people passing by on the pavement outside. Dusk was falling and inside the coffee bar the lighting was soft. In the far corners snoggers sprawled over the easy chairs and cigarette smoke hung in a stationary cloud just below the ceiling.

The jukebox was turned down low, so that you could only just hear Roy Orbison's 'Dream Baby'. On the walls posters were plastered at every angle – the James Mason movie *Lolita* at the Savoy cinema, exhortations to wear a crash helmet when motorcycling and big pictures of Telstar up in space among the stars.

Barry and Terry sat perched on bar stools, elbows wedged on the formica counter, drinking Coke from the bottle. In front of them was a blank wall, but they stared at it as if looking at a view. The two stools on either side of them quickly became occupied by two girls. Both wore tight-fitting jeans and white stilettos, complemented by a high-necked jumper and a bleached-blonde bob with twirly kiss curls at the sides. They could have been twins but they weren't.

Barry and Terry continued their conversation and appeared to be unaware of the girls beside them. This was, however, not so. The two young men raised their eyebrows at each other and winked and jerked their heads to signal their awareness to each other. They drank their Coke and waited for things to happen.

The girl beside Terry leaned across him and eased his bottle to one side: 'So, Tez, still at that slaughterhouse, are you? Haditaways or something, isn't it?' She smiled a bright pink smile, waiting for a reaction.

'Harroway's,' corrected Terry, putting his Coke bottle back in its original position.

The taller girl, who sat next to Barry, placed a hand on his shoulder and said in his ear, 'But you are still killing pigs, aren't you?'

Barry turned to her and thought how attractive she could be without the trowelled makeup. She had green eyes, which he liked, but a cluster of blackheads on her nose, which he did not. 'Yes, we are. What about it?' Barry understood the importance of looking moody and affected a kind of sneer which he felt gave him a Lawrence Harvey look.

The girl beside Terry now leaned right across him as if he no longer existed and cooed to Barry, 'Aah, what a shame for the poor little piggies! Are you sending them up to the piggy heaven?'

'How should I know? I'm not sure they go anywhere, except on your plate.'

'Yuk! That's horrible. When they die, they must go somewhere.'

Barry leaned forward, so that their faces almost met, Terry being squashed out of the picture altogether. Barry was working up to something that had been on his mind for some days: 'Why should they go anywhere at all when they're dead? They're just bags of sloppy stuff and when they're dead, they're dead.'

Still only an inch from his face, the girl said, 'But we don't just finish when we die, do we?'

Barry stared into her eyes and whispered, 'I don't know any more. I think we just die. This heaven and hell stuff is just fairy stories.'

Barry leaned further forward in a clumsy attempt to give her a kiss but she drew her head back and wagged her finger at him, while her friend laughed and lit a cigarette.

It was just before six in the evening on a sultry Tuesday. The trees were in heavy leaf, it was windless and grey clouds held in the clammy heat. The BSA was burbling along the Mellish Road towards the dual carriageway. For Barry and Terry the working day was over. Terry, by now a much more confident pillion passenger, joined his hands behind his back, the way he'd seen leather-clad birds doing it as they posed behind their ton-up boyfriends on their 750s. Even Terry realised a violent bump could pitch him into the road but, for now, appearances had to hold sway over road safety. Because Barry had a passenger behind him, he couldn't stretch out across his maroon machine like a TT rider and felt rather suburban, sitting bolt upright, the flies collecting on his goggles. Fortunately, however, when they arrived at a junction or at traffic lights, he could still indulge in a lot of unnecessary revving in order to attract any passing female attention.

They came to the dual carriageway and Barry opened up the throttle. He began to lean into the corners, unaware that Terry had closed his eyes and was fighting back the urge to bring his arms forward again and grasp Barry round the waist. That way at least they would both be killed together. On their right the Dilke Arms went by and ahead lay the canal bridge.

Terry prodded Barry in his side and Barry tilted his head back to listen. 'How fast are we going, Baz?'

'Fifty-five. I hope you're not shitting yourself on my pillion seat!'

Terry tutted but it was whisked away by the slipstream. Then he shouted, 'I'm just not quite ready to die tonight. I've got fish and chips for tea.'

Barry replied, keeping his eyes on the canal bridge ahead but half turning to Terry, 'Well, we're like the pigs, aren't we, Tez? Just slime and guts is what we are. Do you reckon we would go anywhere?'

'What, you mean like heaven or something like that, or hell in your case?'

'You know what I mean, Tez. Would it be just like switching a light off? Gone, finished.'

Because Barry was taking such a lively interest in this discussion, he failed to decelerate for the bridge and the two young men experienced the concept of weightlessness. They both rose gracefully out of their seats, as the front forks of the BSA telescoped shut, only to land heavily a few seconds later.

'Shit!' breathed Terry. Barry did not turn but he agreed entirely with Terry's assessment.

Terry leaned forward and yelled to Barry, 'We nearly found out that time, Baz! Thank goodness I've got clean underpants on, in case we died.'

'I'd be surprised if they're still clean now!' laughed Barry uneasily, as they approached the junction at the White House.

In no time at all their last day at Harroway's arrived. It was a Friday and the slaughterhouse was busy. A large delivery of pigs waited in the pen. As always, they had an uncanny foreboding about their immediate future. The noise carried for miles on such mornings. They squealed and shrieked and struggled to get out of the pen, many hundreds of them, a pink, heaving mass. They climbed over each other, they trampled on each other, they nipped each other, they fell and disappeared under a mountain of bodies. They became covered in straw, mud and dung. Mr Ralphs would then give the order for the pen to be opened, so that the pigs could be channelled onto the killing floor. Then the noise would rise to an almost painful pitch, as sudden death stepped forward in the shape of the deadly calipers, which would dispatch them to somewhere, or would it? Terry and Barry, engulfed in their working gear, still were not sure. They were no longer distressed by the sights and sounds before them, yet this in itself was of concern to both.

Their task on this final day was to work in the 'head department'. As its macabre name suggests, pigs' heads were stacked high in this narrow, stuffy room. Without ceremony, the heads were tossed to the top of the pile either by their ears or by two fingers up the snout. Barry stacked the heads, while Terry loaded them on to a trolley and wheeled them away for processing.

The floor became slippery with blood and slime. Several times Barry sluiced it with buckets of water, as he had been trained to do. Still his boots lost purchase and he slid about like an oddly clad skater, flailing for a hand hold.

The inevitable happened. Barry went down with a thud. He fell on his side and it hurt. But this was not the memory that was to stay with him for the rest of his life. He fell, so that his face was no more than an inch away from one of the pigs' heads. The head lay on its side at the bottom of the pile so that, from where Barry was lying, winded, it was staring, open-eyed, straight at him. Its little eyes were open and glared malevolently at helpless Barry, who could not even draw breath. For long seconds youth and pig stared at each other. For Barry it seemed quite impossible that this detached head could be sightless, seeing nothing, feeling nothing, thinking nothing. He was certain it still had a life of its own. Its expression was one of utter contempt for this pathetic individual who was a party to its untimely death and that of so many hundreds of its fellows. How it hated Barry! How, if only it had a body, it would lunge at him and make him pay for the insensitivity he had learnt. Barry was a killer, a killer of pigs, a slaughterer. Now he was faced with the enormity of what he was doing. This head could see him, this snout could smell him, this half-shut mouth could taste his sweat. Some sort of contact had been made, Barry knew, and he didn't like it, it made him uneasy, he somehow felt as though he had been forced to look at himself.

'Barry, Barry, Earth calling Barry, are you receiving? Over.' Jo Enoch looked despairingly at her husband, who seemed to be away with the fairies. He had his knife and fork in his hands but he was gazing into space, somewhere far away. Slowly he turned to his wife and blinked his eyes into focus, placing his cutlery gently and deliberately on the breakfast plate. 'Crikey, Barry, where did you go to?'

'Nowhere special. It would take too long to explain and you've heard it before, countless times.'

Jo glanced at him knowingly, pulled up a chair and sat down beside him. 'Since Terry Ballinger died last year you've been back to that slaughterhouse too many times in your mind. It always gets you low.'

As he rose from the table, Barry murmured, 'I'll just go upstairs and have a wash.' Once in the bathroom, he splashed some cold water on his face and reached blindly for the towel. He stood in front of the big mirror and patted his face dry. Then he looked at himself and saw himself looking back. He thought about his old friend of so many years and whispered to his reflection, 'Rest in peace, Terence, old son.' He continued to stare at his reflection and from long ago that same unease stole across his mind. He made his way shakily downstairs, gripping the banister.

The Farm Stop

The third year in grammar school has been quite good so far. The only really serious bit has been the fag of having to choose options. Those are the subjects we want to specialise in as we go towards GCE, that's the General Certificate of Education.

Now, I quite like school but what I like a whole lot more is the quid I get paid by Mr Davies for my Saturday stint on his fruit and veg van. He's a gen bloke and I get free fags on the job – well, not exactly, that is, he doesn't give them to me, I sort of – well, you know. My dad would call it 'evil opportunism'. If it's there, you take it. I'm sure I shall grow out of it. It's like chucking litter. Why do I chuck litter? I don't know. I'm a clean and tidy person. It beats me. I think deep down I want to be a beatnik but it's not really my bag, if you see what I mean.

My Saturdays with Mr Davies run to a regular pattern. I spend my day in the back, serving the ladies, sweeping up or just hanging on for dear life while Mr Davies drives the old heap from one stop to the next round my part of the West Midlands. I don't get a lunch break as such but around midday, when I've been working for a good five hours, he stops near Barr Beacon. Old Scott Farm is below the level of the lane, almost hidden in trees, although the front door is visible a few yards away. It's quite a low whitewashed place with small windows and tiny panes of glass in thick walls, like part of an old castle. Mr Davies pulls in on the grassy verge and I get an hour to myself while he talks to the farmer's wife. God knows what they find to talk about. Sounds really boring, doesn't it?

My name's Keith, by the way. I should have told you that before. Grown-ups like to know kids' names. My surname's Golder. At school they call me Goldilocks, daft really, because my hair isn't gold and I haven't got three bears.

I remember the first time we pulled in for the hour at Old Scott Farm. It was grey and cold, the trees were bare and Mr Davies was well wrapped up to the neck in his brown cow gown, his muffler and his flat cap. His cap was so tatty and greasy that it had no colour at all. I suppose it had also been brown at some time. There was a big black smudge in the middle of the peak where he kept pulling it down. He had big toe-capped shoes that were always covered in the dust from the sacks and soil off the potatoes. But he was always clean-shaven when I worked with him and used to check himself in the wing mirror of the van before he went off to see Mrs Roddick. That first day I noticed it especially, because he didn't seem the sort of bloke to bother about what he looked like. In any case, when you're that old, what does it matter?

'Now, son, you pick up that bloody broom and move it round the van so quick it becomes a bloody blur, an instrument of cleanliness. You've complained all morning about the cold, so now you can warm your bloody self up!'

I wasn't at all put off by this, because he was quite a kind man and I knew he quite liked me.

'Yes, Mr Davies. How long will you be?'

'I'll be gone an hour, lad, not that it's any of your business, you nosy little sod. Mrs Roddick and I are old friends. Known each other for donkeys' years, we have, and on a Saturday we like to have a little chat.'

'What, every Saturday?'

'Yes, lad, every bloody Saturday, if that's all right with you?'

I mumbled that it was okay with me, even if it did seem a total waste of time and a boring way to spend an hour.

'Do you get a cup of tea?' I enquired tentatively.

'Yes, I do.'

'Do you think she would give me...' By shaking my head, I recovered quite quickly from the slap that landed on it.

'I've told you to mind your business and sweep this van. If there was a prize for being a lazy bleeder, then you'd get it.'

It crossed my mind to thank him for this compliment but I decided against it. His hands were huge calloused things and could really hurt.

Mr Davies opened the driver's door of the cab, stood on the step and gave two blasts on the horn. A flight of bedraggled crows rose from the bare treetops, calling their protests, and then it was quiet again. Then, as Mr Davies and I stood beside the van, the flaky wooden front door of the farmhouse was pushed open with some difficulty, scraping and juddering, until in the doorway stood Mrs Roddick, the farmer's wife. I don't mind telling you I always had a mental picture of what a farmer's wife should look like – plump and cheerful, grey hair in a bun, holding a tray loaded with homemade cakes. Not this farmer's wife! Standing in the doorway was a slim brunette, she would be forty-something, I don't know about people of that age but a lot younger than Mr Davies. She was wearing a pale green jumper with a V-neck and tight-fitting jeans. I noticed that her feet were bare, she was smoking a cigarette and there was music coming from inside the house – I think it was one of the Trad Jazz bands, like Kenny Ball or Acker Bilk.

'Crikey!' I whispered.

'Exactly,' said Mr Davies, 'and she's a widow, lad. So get sweeping and have this van shipshape by the time I get back.'

As he walked away across the lane and down the little path, I started wondering what the importance was of her being a widow. Why would he tell me that?

During my hour I lit a stub of cigarette out of my tin and started sweeping out the back of the van. I had a swig of stewed tea from my thermos and then scrambled about, picking up potatoes and tidying up all the vegetables. I was quite proud of how the van looked after all this. I had even polished the stainless-steel scale pan, a detail which I intended to point out to Mr Davies, who must have been quite bored by now, talking for nearly an hour and drinking tea and I'm not too keen on jazz anyway.

Well, after exactly an hour, the flaky old door of the farmhouse scraped open again and in the doorway I could see part of Mr Davies. For a moment I thought he was giving Mrs Roddick a hug, but why would he do that? He knew he would see her next

Saturday. Then the door scraped open a little wider. Yes, it was Kenny Ball in the background. Mr Davies had his cow gown on and the top two buttons of his shirt open and he was using a handkerchief to mop his bald head. I suppose Mrs Roddick kept her house pretty warm. As Mr Davies made his way up the steep path, he seemed to be breathing heavily and puffed out his cheeks with each step. His face was very red and shone like a lamp in the nippy air.

'Are you all right, Mr Davies?'

'Just let me get my breath back, son, and I'll have a look round the back of the van.'

He leaned a heavy hand on my shoulder and stood puffing and panting, clouds of steam gathering around his head and shoulders. When he seemed to have recovered, he clambered into the back of the van and made some approving noises, finally turning to me.

'Well done, son,' he said, 'you're more use than I gave you credit for.'

'Does Mrs Roddick want any fruit or veg?'

'No, lad, she doesn't,' he said as he walked towards the little opening that led into the cab. I followed him and leaned inside, while he lowered himself into the driver's seat and took his muffler off.

'Does she ever have anything from the van?'

'Sometimes she does and sometimes she doesn't, is that good enough for you?'

'Do you think she'll want something next week, like some spuds or...'

Mr Davies turned his bull neck round to me and whipped his flat cap off: 'Look, she might want something next time but she doesn't want anything this time. Is that clear?'

'Yes, Mr Davies.'

Mr Davies reached down for the starter button and, as he was leaning forward, muttered, 'She's had all she's likely to get, has Mrs Roddick.'

What on earth did he mean by that? The whole thing was most odd.

When we'd got under way and we were bowling along towards Great Barr along the narrow lane, I leaned forward into the cab and said to Mr Davies, 'You like her, don't you?'

'Like who?'

'You like Mrs Roddick, don't you?' Mr Davies stared straight ahead through the dirty old windscreen and lit a Woodbine. 'I saw you with your arms round her.'

Mr Davies cleared his throat and drew on his cigarette: 'She's an old friend, son. I like her well enough. You'll understand when you're a bit older.'

I thought about this as I grasped my handhold: 'Well, maybe she'll have something next Saturday.'

'Aye lad, maybe she will.'

I always had a 'short back and sides'. In those days that's what every boy had. I went to my dad's barber, Reg Woollaston Gents' Hairdresser, in Station Road. My dad would sit behind me with the other men all in a row, some reading the sports pages, some smoking a pipe or a cigarette and some staring at the back of my young neck, eager to make witty comments. A boy of eleven, sitting in a high chair, having his hair cut, is an easy target. Mr Woollaston's busy hands would click and buzz around my head, followed by the inevitable dollop of Brylcreem to finish the process. I loved the smell of Brylcreem. Mr Woollaston would massage it into my scalp, his movements jerking my head this way and that and then pulling it back so that suddenly I was staring at the strip light.

It was a Wednesday in the Christmas holidays. Mr Woollaston closed his shop at one o'clock, because it was early closing day on Wednesdays. My dad was still on holiday and was sitting behind me, waiting his turn. There were several other men also hoping to be attended to before the shop closed. Mr Woollaston was in a hurry and was being unusually rough with me. He caught my ear with the comb. My hand flew up from underneath the white smock and I began rubbing the injured area.

'What's the matter, son, have I cut your ear off?' Mr Woollaston flicked the comb against the back of my head.

My dad roared with laughter and slapped his knees, 'You might as well cut them both off, Reg, he never bloody listens to anybody in any case!'

The fat man with the curved pipe chipped in, 'He's a sensitive boy, that's what the trouble is.'

'Sensitive? I'll give him sensitive! According to his father,' here Mr Woollaston turned to look at my dad, 'he's nothing but a layabout. I don't know about sensitive.'

My head turned from one to the other as far as it would reach.

Then the man in the donkey jacket with sort of Teddy-boy hair said, 'Leave him alone, you lot, he looks normal to me.'

'Normal!' scoffed my dad, 'if my lad's normal, I'm a Dutchman.' This struck me as odd, since my dad had never mentioned this before. He had always told me he came from Norwich. Still, I suppose that's on the way to Holland.

When Mr Woollaston had finished with me, he undid the smock, whisked it aside, shouting 'Olé!' I had no idea what he meant by that and just smiled weakly.

As he helped me down from the chair, he bent down and, looking me straight in the eye, enquired, 'Something for the weekend, sir?' The whole shop erupted into laughter.

I stood there, in front of six men, my head resplendent with Brylcreem, my arms dangling, and stammered, 'How do you mean, Mr Woollaston?'

The Teddy boy spoke again, 'Leave the kid alone, Reg. If he wants something for the weekend, he'll ask for it.'

Later, when I asked my dad what I could possibly want for the weekend, he suggested I should shut up and mind my own business. It was an adult's joke and not intended for me. If it wasn't intended for me, why did he ask me? When you're eleven, life still holds many mysteries.

By 1966 I was growing my hair and had eschewed the services of Reg Woollaston long before. My hair was over my collar and flicked up in a kind of curl at the back, which I thought quite rakish. My dad told me I looked like a 'nancy' and it would serve me right if I was expelled from school.

My best friend was Dougie Lote, a tall, thin youth with long greasy hair and a slight limp. I remember that at junior school Dougie had worn one of those awful leg-irons. Dougie looked like a tall, oily version of Adam Faith, yet his main obsession was the works of William Shakespeare, from which he would quote liberally. Shakespeare with a Black Country accent has a special quality and sounds somehow more evocative. If he could think of no appropriate quotation, he would invent one, using his own knowledge of Shakespearean English.

My own obsession was Rita Smee, a girl in my class, or rather a goddess who swept into the classroom to join us ordinary mortals as a favour. Rita was a popular girl, which was an obstacle in itself. She had many admirers, ranging from sixth formers like film stars to kids in my own year with half-broken voices that bleated like goats on a hillside. Rita had wavy, golden hair gathered into a long ponytail. She moved with a languorous sway of her hips and carried her school bag in front of her, clasped to her bosom like a baby. How I longed to be that school bag! I had about as much chance of that as of being elected form captain.

At morning break on a warm Tuesday, feeling reckless to the point of elation, I accidentally-on-purpose brushed past Rita Smee. Fighting the urge to swoon with passion at her feet, I asked, 'Do you want to go out with me, Rita?'

Rita turned to me, as her gorgeous retinue of girlfriends stood around expectantly. 'Why would I want to do that, Leon?'

The other girls smirked to each other with lowered eyelids. Here was a question I hadn't anticipated, assuming the reason was obvious. It wasn't.

'Erm – I've got some good records back at my pad.' Pad sounded good. I was pleased with pad.

Rita turned her enormous blue eyes on me and, as if addressing a lower form of life asked, 'Oh really? What would those be, seventy-eights?' Her friends laughed, as I compressed my lips and fought the urge to run away.

I stood my ground and made a move I hadn't thought of before. It involved lying to Rita but what the hell! I had to persuade her to go out with me against all the odds. I opened my mouth and out tumbled this statement: 'I've got *Aftermath*.' I awaited the reaction.

Rita's eyes opened even wider, difficult but true. 'You've got *Aftermath*? The Rolling Stones? Just released? With "Mother's Little Helper"?'

'The same. If you come round to my place I'll play it for you as many times as you like.' I could tell she was thinking about it. I watched her tits rise and fall several times. She looked at her beautiful friends and her beautiful friends looked back at her.

'Leon, if I come over to yours and I find you haven't got *Aftermath* at all and you've lied to me, you'll be sorry.'

'I have got it, I swear to you. I'll fix a date with you, so you can come and hear it.'

'Not so fast, Leon, show it to me first.'

'I'm not bringing it to school, so I'll ride past your place tomorrow night and show you I've got it.'

Now I really was in a predicament. I knew only one person on earth who already had the *Aftermath* LP by the Rolling Stones. That person was Dougie Lote.

The following evening at about six o'clock found me standing outside the Lote household. The low evening sunshine bathed Dougie's face, as he stood outside his front door, with a large slice of toast and Marmite protruding from his mouth. He had been using the slice of toast doubled over as a beak, and had been making quacking noises and flapping his arms, asking me what animal he was supposed to be.

'Dougie, you don't understand the seriousness of this situation. I need to borrow that LP sleeve right now and ride past Rita's, waving it like a banner.'

Dougie finally finished his piece of toast and, squinting in the golden light, said, 'Festers, Leon, I don't know whether I feel like letting you borrow *Aftermath*. It cost me a lot of money.'

'But Dougie, Rita will come to my place Saturday night if she thinks I've got that LP.'

'Methinks thou dost protest too much, Leon. What do I get in return?'

'Twenty Stuyvesant, your favourites. And don't tell a soul the LP belongs to you.'

'Leon, you have a deal and I will hold my peace. Otherwise I really would be a blackguard who dare scarce show his face upon the mart.'

As we stood in the warm sunshine, Dougie picking bits of toast from between his teeth, my happiness was complete. I was already fantasising about doing unmentionable things with Rita Smee and hearing her voice purring, 'Leon, Leon.'

Later that evening I sat in Dougie's lounge with *Aftermath* playing in the background. The track was 'Flight 505', to which Dougie was miming, using a torch and shining the light into his face to give him the illusion of spotlights. Abruptly he broke off and asked, 'So she came out and saw the LP sleeve. What happened then?'

'She opened her front door and gave me a thumbs up,' I said.

'Festers!' exclaimed Dougie, 'is that all? Doth nought else transpire? Cometh the damsel fair to thine abode for a shag?'

'I hope so,' I said, 'I've gone to enough trouble. I want you to lend me the LP before Saturday. I'll come down here with the Styves and pick it up.'

'That will be most meet, old fruit. I wish thee well with thine fornication. It's true Rita hath a bounteous aspect in all her parts.'

Lesson changeovers were chaos. Somehow they were worse on Fridays than on other days. The cramped, two-way traffic of hundreds of young bodies would pass along the narrow corridors and stairways in a bid to get from one lesson to the next. Every few yards a member of staff, black like a raven in his gown, would be seen, swept along by the tide. Fridays lent an added desperation to this mass movement. It was as if everyone wanted to get through the motions as hurriedly as possible and then be off home.

I vividly remember craning my neck above the heads, in order to catch Dougie coming the other way towards the metalwork shop, clad in his faded, dark blue apron with its kangaroo-pouch pocket at the front. Long before I actually saw him, I could hear his voice ringing out above the other voices in a raucous Australian accent, as he hopped along, pretending to be a kangaroo. His limp made the hopping all the more grotesque, more like a gremlin than a kangaroo. Not far behind me was Mr Savage, who I knew would not be best pleased if I were to hold everyone up in order to enjoy exchanging a few words with Dougie Lote. Still, sometimes risks have to be taken, don't they?

Just as Dougie was passing, I tugged the sleeve of his shirt and said, 'You know it has to be tonight, Dougie. I'll bring the twenty Styves and you lend me *Aftermath* till Sunday.'

'Bonzer, cobber, fair dinkum, sport! Something for the weekend, eh?'

My mind flew back to Reg Woollaston's stuffy barber's shop, the tufts of hair of every hue scattered about across the linoleum floor, the cigarette and pipe smoke floating near the ceiling and the busy clicking of the scissors.

'Leon Bennett! Move on, you cretinous boy! You're blocking half the corridor, and of all the boys you choose to talk to, it has to be that half-wit Lote. Now move!'

So the deal was done.

By the time Saturday evening arrived, I was light-headed with anticipation. To think that Rita Smee would actually be coming to our house, would stand in our lounge, would sit in one of our chairs. How many times had I popped upstairs to the bathroom to check my hair? Was it sufficiently scruffy? Could I persuade her that I was a sort of dropout, a colourful rebel, the sort of boy she'd want to know? Did my skin look too soft, too suburban, too adolescent? I wanted it to look weather-beaten and rugged, the skin of a well-travelled young man. But from out of the mirror there stared a scrawny, pasty-faced, spotty teenager who knew nothing about the real world. Still, I could only do my best. I'd got her to visit the house and that was a start.

When the doorbell went, my stomach lurched sideways and I cleared my throat several times to try to make my voice deeper. As I approached the front door, I attempted a kind of swagger, swinging my shoulders and sneering with one side of my mouth. With a trembling hand I turned the doorknob and opened the door. There stood Rita Smee, the ultimate vision of teenage sexuality. Her hair, which was not quite blonde, was out of its usual ponytail and fell over her shoulders, heavily back-combed. She wore a white, high-necked sweater, so tight that I could picture her naked. Her black miniskirt was so painfully short that I almost had to grit my teeth to avoid staring at it. Her boots were black and shiny and came up to her knees.

'Hello, Rita, come on in.' I stepped back and made a weak, floppy gesture with my hand.

'What's wrong with your face, Leon?'

'Erm, how do you mean?' I bleated, my voice cracking because I'd pitched it too low.

'You seem to be sneering and your voice is funny.' She swayed inside and I thought to myself, be normal, Leon, and don't try any more tough-guy stuff. It doesn't work and Rita thinks you're a twit.

We went into our little lounge and Rita slid her bag off her shoulder. The room was filled with her perfume.

'Mind if I smoke a ciggie?' She extracted a long king-size from the packet of twenty and eased it between her lips as if performing a sexual act on it.

I already had the *Aftermath* LP playing at low volume on the record player. I increased the volume to give a more clubby atmosphere. Rita put her fingers in her ears, 'God, Leon, I'm not deaf! You don't need to blast us both out of the room.' Then she gave me a second look and asked suspiciously, 'Why are the curtains drawn in here? It's not even dark yet.' I hadn't expected that and some quick thinking was called for.

'It's to keep the room warm and give more privacy.' I smiled at her in what I thought was a masterful way.

She frowned back. 'Privacy for what, Leon? What were you planning to do?'

'Erm, nothing.'

Bloody hell! I was furious with myself. How stupid and how weak was that! It simply invited Rita's sarcastic response, 'Nothing? It's going to be a spaz evening then. I've come here to dance.'

My mind flailed about, as I struggled to get to grips with this unexpected information. I looked at Rita, carefully avoiding her breasts. She met my gaze and went on, 'Yes, I really want to dance to *Aftermath*. I'm a very keen dancer and I want you to dance with me, Leon. I'd feel a right berk dancing on my own.'

My emotions were confused at this. I must admit that the idea of dancing in a small private room with Rita did attract me. But somehow I could not erase from my mind the vision of her lying on the carpet with her legs in the air. Looking back, if she had in fact suggested that, I would have been at a total loss. But boys thrive on fantasy and anticipation.

'Okay, Rita, that's fine by me. I'm not a bad dancer. Let's get started.'

So we danced all evening, moving separately for the first half hour, until at last Rita took my hands and we started dancing together. It wasn't a clinch, it was quite chaste, with a little gap between us, though our hands were joined. Then, after a few more minutes, she drew me closer to her and placed my hands on her hips, while her own were clasped around the back of my neck. Paradise! I was surprised how good it felt. Rita had her eyes closed and twice I bumped into her chest quite hard. I felt I should apologise and did so.

Rita opened her eyes and said to me, 'They're very firm, aren't they, Leon?'

'Erm, erm, yes – very nice, Rita. You are very nice all over.'

Rita told me she was enjoying the evening and didn't mind that I'd squashed against her. Then she said, 'Leon, if I tell you something, will you promise me to keep it to yourself?'

I assured her she need have no worries on that score.

Looking me straight in the eye, she whispered, 'They're falsies, Leon, I'm really flat-chested.'

'Well, I think you look fab, Rita, and I really fancy you.'

We continued in this way for some time. I felt quite heady with her perfume, which she told me was called Intimate. It is a smell I still remember today and will never forget. Then Rita glanced over my shoulder, as we danced past the record player, on the closed lid of which lay the *Aftermath* LP sleeve, face down.

'What's that?' she asked, craning over my shoulder.

'What's what?'

'What's that, what's that writing on the record sleeve?'

Before I could stop her, she swept the LP cover off the lid of the record player and scrutinised it, holding it by the side of my head. 'Leon, this says "Property of D. Lote". This record isn't yours at all, is it?'

Until now, my normal practice, when in a corner like this, had been to lie my way out. However preposterous my excuse or explanation, I would deliver it with bare-faced panache. But I had learnt something from Rita that evening and I went for total candour. I stopped dancing, held her by the shoulders, and made eye contact with her: 'No, it's not mine, it's Dougie's. I borrowed it because I know you like it. I would do a lot more than that to get you to spend an evening with me.'

Rita smiled and took my hands in hers: 'But you didn't know I wanted to dance all evening, did you, Leon? Are you fed up with me?'

Again I considered what I had learnt that evening and was completely open: 'I've had a great evening, Rita, and I don't care whether we snog or dance.'

My reward was a kiss on the lips and several more during the walk back to Rita's place in the dark. We agreed we would start going out together and I was as happy as Larry, despite total ignorance of who that lucky man actually was.

At half eleven on Sunday morning I knocked on Dougie's front door, brandishing his LP in my hand, so that he would see it through the rippled glass. The door burst open and Dougie pushed out his head and shoulders. I was not astonished to find him with a black patch over one eye and a fake beard drawn on his face, reeking of Cherry Blossom shoe polish.

'Well met, sirrah! How went the evening? Didst thou penetrate the damsel?'

Although I understood the gist of this, I was in no mood for it. Rather gruffly, I replied, 'We had a great evening and thanks for the LP, and no, I didn't do any penetrating.'

In astonishment, Dougie raised his black patch and pulled it outwards on its elastic. 'Indeed it pains me to learn thy tidings, o bungle-brain! Still, it is of no import. How passed the hours?'

It gave me great satisfaction to see Dougie suddenly lose his grip on the eye-patch, whereupon it slapped against his right eye, causing him to yelp in pain. I handed over the LP, while Dougie squinted at it and pulled a variety of suffering faces.

I told him, 'We danced all evening and it was really great. Rita and I are going out together, starting tonight. It's all thanks to you, Dougie, and to the Rolling Stones.'

Dougie proceeded to fan his injured eye with the LP sleeve, having removed the patch, and beamed at me: 'Danced? Still, a shag by any other name would smell as sweet! No doubt thou willst receive thy pound of flesh from Mistress Smee in due course.'

'No doubt I will, Dougie, but thanks to you I've already had something for the weekend.'

Wetton Mill

Of course Neil had no idea that, by the time he was thirty, he would be completely bald. He had thin, light brown hair with a bit of a wave in it and grey eyes, quite steely he thought, which he used to fix upon the girls, as if to bore through them like a gimlet.

Apart from his eyes, he possessed a deep, resonant voice which somehow forced people to listen to him. It was a voice older than his twenty years, one that might have belonged to a bank manager or a solicitor. Not that he talked posh, in fact there was a clear trace of Chasetown in his speech, a solid connection to Highfields Road where he lived. It was its low pitch which struck you at first. He would sit astride his Vespa and place his feet on either side with great precision, rather like an athlete preparing to throw a javelin, and would growl, 'Bugger this bloody thing!' as he knocked one of his forest of wing mirrors out of place. For Neil, being a Mod was a serious business, yet more of a prescription for fashion and style than an excuse to go out and look for violence. Getting his parka dirty in a fight was unthinkable.

Yet Neil was far from shallow. He would never choose his friends according to whether they belonged to the Mod or Rocker camp. His friends were his friends regardless and his best friend, John, had long hair and a 350cc BSA, which he rode in black leathers complete with fringes, a silver crash helmet and a white handkerchief, knotted at the back, covering his nose and mouth. John looked like a cross between a cattle rustler from the Old West and John Surtees, the motorcycling icon of the time. Neil was without doubt the tougher of the two, tough in his convictions and pig-headed in his small-mining-town values. John was taller and appeared more threatening but was quite dependent on his friend for suggestions and ideas.

They did a lot of things together and had a laugh as young men do, falling about when one of them farted and making comments about the breasts of some unfortunate girl in a news-agent's where Neil had bought twenty Players. John smoked occasionally but, being insecure, was far more cautious of himself and more restrained in everything he did. He had that 'retention of self' which leads to the enjoyment of life being postponed and having to be played back in hindsight. Neil enjoyed his life, while John viewed the movie at a later date, often years afterwards.

Neil was quite clear that he enjoyed John's company and would ride all the way to Two Gates to see him. John was less inclined to reciprocate, not because he liked Neil any the less, but simply because of the lower value he placed upon himself. He would never call unannounced on his friend, because of a vague anxiety about rejection by Neil's parents or by Neil himself; perhaps it was their mealtime or perhaps they were having a family discussion, something which, in fact, the Palmer-Whites were unlikely to do. This was another symptom of John's slight withdrawal from a world in which he longed to be at ease.

John counted Neil a very important friend, although he frequently struggled with the urge to be alone and not to mix at all. This feeling plagues that type of youth, as if he needs a script in order to interact with others, as if by being spontaneous, he may let himself down or, even worse, accidentally reveal his true self. It is that very true self that people like John strive to keep locked in darkness, like someone relieving himself in the privy, when suddenly the door is opened and they are caught with their trousers round their ankles. John tried to be what he felt people expected him to be. He strove to build up an image of himself, complete with idiosyncrasies, which would be acceptable to others. Many years later he would be able to drop this guard and show himself as he really was, but for now it had to remain firmly in place. Like a delicate plant, he had to grow behind the shelter of a wall.

John felt he was some sort of Rocker, though he hated oil and grease and even shrank from pulling the petrol tap on his motorbike, because it made his fingers smell of petrol and sometimes smeared dirt on them. But he liked the image of the independent knight of the road, cavalier with the girls and friendly yet casually dismissive towards other males. He looked the part and he carried it well. He was a good actor and would portray movements and gestures he'd seen in the movies or on TV. His notion of masculinity was borrowed from Patrick Allen, Patrick Macnee and even Marlon Brando. It's not easy to appear to be rebellious and aggressive, yet at ease at the same time. John could do this provided things ran smoothly. If he ran out of petrol or had a puncture, Marlon Brando would rapidly turn into something more like Charlie Drake or Stan Laurel.

'Do you want to go somewhere tomorrow? Unless you want to go to church, as it's Sunday.' Neil fixed him with that stare and sparked up, squinting with one eye.

'You know I don't believe in God and neither do you. We could go up to Derbyshire. We've talked about it but never done it. Do you think that Mod contraption of yours would make it up the hills?'

'It pulls more totty than that smoky lump of grease that you sit on. I'll plan a route and you can come to mine for about ten.'

'Why should I have to come to yours?'

'Because my place is on the way, you daft sod.'

John considered this for a while, not sufficiently sure of the geography of the Midlands to challenge his friend. In any case, Neil with a fag on always looked very adult and not to be toyed with. John agreed to come to Highfields Road, Chasetown, the following morning and did a swift mental calculation about how much petrol he would need. Neil always appeared to have more money, it was a knack he had, in fact he had The Knack generally.

Noisily they rattled and bumped north up the A515 towards Ashbourne. John's telescopic front forks dived and bounced beneath his arms and the regular drumming of his exhaust lulled him into a kind of dream, as trees swished overhead and oncoming traffic flashed past with a sound like the beating of a giant bird's wing. He squinted through his visor at Neil, the Mod, his hair rippling in the slipstream, his parka billowing as though a third person were struggling to get out. There rode his friend, crouched on his Vespa, there to spend the day with him. Neil was only on this road on his scooter because of their friendship. John watched the scooter buzzing ahead, its little wheels stumbling into every pothole, but still Neil rode on to spend the day with his friend.

John thought about the odd sense of responsibility he felt, being the reason Neil was here, riding through potholes, heading for Ashbourne. If John had turned down this trip, he would probably have his head stuck in an atlas on an imaginary journey, almost certainly by Boeing 707, crossing an ocean to somewhere where there were palm trees and ceiling fans. But he was doing this to please Neil and because he would never undertake such a ride on his own.

He fantasised about Neil turning round in the road and heading off back to Chasetown. Why would he not do that? Because he was his friend and because he was deliberately spending time with him. John knew that Neil would never entertain such thoughts. For Neil the situation was straightforward – John was his mate and together they were on a ride to Wetton Mill. He would have no mental struggles about why his friend was here and John knew full well his friend's only thought right now was when he should pull off and light up.

They stopped just north of Draycott-in-the-Clay and propped their machines up by the roadside. They stood side by side with their backs to the traffic, peeing into a low hawthorn hedge, a quiet sense of camaraderie prevailing. Neil puffed on his cigarette, one eye screwed up, his head tilted backwards, showing his enjoyment of the warm weather and the North Staffordshire countryside.

John pondered whether it was unnatural to stand beside another bloke who was peeing. How would they appear to passing motorists? He was much taller than Neil and clad in leathers. Did he look ridiculous? Neil's clothes always seemed to sit on him more easily, he had a certain style about the way he wore things. John knew he could get off with as many girls as Neil but his own clothes hung more awkwardly, as if on a wooden frame, and his own style was more quirky, even eccentric. John suspected very strongly that he would not come into his own until he was fifty and then he would somehow grow into his body and grow into himself. But youth was just right for Neil, who seemed always at ease.

'Do you know, I can hear that bloody motorbike behind me all the time?'

John looked at him, slightly hurt, not at all the way a biker should feel: 'Then I'll ride in front until we get to Wetton Mill. I'll set the pace now and you can attempt to follow.' He smiled in a lopsided way. That was more like the behaviour of a biker, more arrogant, coming out with throwaway lines.

'Attempt? You cheeky shit! I should have peed on your boots.' Neil laughed and suddenly looked far too young to be smoking and riding a Vespa. John laughed too and felt a thrill at how much he enjoyed the insult. It felt like total acceptance into some kind of group world.

They made a satisfying noise through the narrow streets of Ashbourne, climbing steeply towards the north end of the town, quite unaware of what an unlikely pair they looked. Neil, who was bent over his scooter to extract every ounce of power from it, was thinking about his girlfriend, Lynn. She lived in Cheslyn Hay and Neil spent a disproportionate amount of time imagining her naked. He had not achieved this yet in reality, but Neil was a person who believed that almost anything was possible and that he could make it happen.

John often noticed with envy how Neil never held back, whatever the situation, and behaved as if clad in invisible armour. Not that John was short of girlfriends, quite the contrary, though he presented himself to the opposite sex in a very different way. John saw himself as a sort of vulnerable, tragic hero, like a Romantic poet, a Byron, a Keats or a Lamartine. He liked the way in which they tended to be tall and emaciated, pale and haunted – except for Byron, obviously. They always seemed to be standing on top of a crag with the wind blowing their long hair and, of course, they all seemed to take drugs. John did not take drugs but always made out that he did. He was afraid of the damage to himself and guessed he would be quick to grow dependent.

Neil was much more forthright about drug abuse and about the people who took drugs. 'Bunch of wankers.' That was Neil's summary and he had no desire to ally himself with such sad weaklings. Young blokes with long hair were pansies, though he made an exception in John's case.

This vulnerability of John's was a very effective ploy, for it was a ploy, something which was truly a part of him yet which he was able to milk when the circumstances were right. He would drop the tough-guy image and immediately turn into a tortured and damaged being. He found that girls were intrigued by this and he learned to switch from one persona to the other at will.

Once they were back on the open road, John decelerated to bring himself abreast of Neil. Neil raised a hand to the side of his mouth and yelled, 'Six and a half miles. Nearly there.'

John knew better than to spend time wondering how his friend could be so precise. If Neil said six and a half miles, then six and a half miles it was. Neil would have an overview of the route in his mind and could memorise an ordnance survey map in the same way that John could recite by heart the label on a bottle of HP Sauce in French. 'Horses for courses' Neil would say, whatever that meant. Perhaps Neil was a betting man, thought John, leaning flat across his bike as they passed a group of girls. This was to give an impression of speed, though the girls, all walkers with backpacks, were far too busy pointing at a hillside to notice either of the intrepid riders.

At Wetton Mill they found a sloping field with a dry-stone wall at the top and a clutch of tents of different shapes and sizes at the bottom. There were also trees at the bottom end, which suggested a brook for the campers.

John and Neil spluttered along a beaten track in first gear, finally stopped their engines and heaved their machines onto the stands. When John pulled off his helmet and lowered his face mask, he was struck by the silence and the smells of warm grass and sheep droppings. Neil stretched and ran both hands through his hair to untangle it, sniffed the air and immediately extracted a crumpled cigarette.

John looked about him, almost overwhelmed by a sense of well-being. Neil's cigarette smoke curled into the summer air and for a long moment neither of them spoke a word. John sat on the grass, breathing in the greasy warmth from his engine and listening to the pings and clicks it gave off as it cooled down. He knew instinctively that this was a special moment in his life, a perfect time and one that he would savour in later years. Even when you are young, you can have a special knowledge of this. It's just something you know.

But the challenge for John was to savour it now, like sucking on a lollipop, rather than postponing it until he could look back in the privacy of his own bedroom at home. John had a sort of inbuilt inhibitor, which prevented him from throwing himself into anything. He had no 'abandon'; instead he had a sort of 'governor', as coaches and lorries have to prevent the driver from putting his foot down too hard. John held himself back in every aspect of his life, as if he would rather watch a movie of himself than engage in real events.

Neil turned and looked down at him. 'Nice here, isn't it, mate? Got to mind the sheep shit though. You don't want that stuck on your bloody leather trousers!'

John squinted up at his friend, because practical considerations had come into his head, pushing the philosophy to one side: 'I hope I've got enough petrol to get back. I put two gallons in but it doesn't seem to have lasted.'

'We're on a slope, you spaz. You can't trust your fuel gauge on a slope.' Neil exhaled smoke noisily, shaking his head in despair at his friend's ignorance. Then, as an afterthought, he smirked, 'I wonder if there's any rumpo in those tents. We should go and have a shufti, old son.'

John was still preoccupied with his fuel status and got up to take hold of his handlebars and shake his bike to listen to the sloshing of the fuel inside the tank. 'Doesn't sound like much in there.' He unscrewed the petrol cap.

Neil pulled a face and tutted, 'I hope you're not going to spend all afternoon belly-aching about your bloody petrol.'

Neil was wearing that expression that preceded some decisive course of action. When he had this look about him, he would normally say, 'Give it here,' to demonstrate that he was about to take control of the whole situation. He would then snatch from John whatever object was causing indecision and deliver a rapid solution. Now, his stub of cigarette smouldering in the corner of his mouth and one eye creased against the smoke, Neil strode over to the BSA and pushed John's hands from the handlebars.

'Give it here, Johnny, I'll sort this out for you.'

John compressed his lips into an irritated line and stepped back from his bike to allow the genius to take over. So annoyed was he, that he turned away with his hands thrust sulkily into the two side pockets of his leather bomber jacket. As he walked away, kicking the dried sheep droppings to one side, he heard Neil's voice behind him, obviously trying to regain his attention.

'Right, old son, let's have a look at this petrol situation.'

John had no idea what made him turn at that moment but something did. It was something to do with Neil and his cigarette. John stopped in mid-stride and turned round to behold Neil slowly lowering his head over the open petrol filler. John could smell the vapour even from where he was standing and, as if in a dream, he saw the glowing fag-end descending. A piece of hot ash falling into the tank would ignite the whole lot. It could happen at any second. Neil would probably turn into a living torch or be blown to pieces.

John found he was unable to speak. He couldn't cry out and for a split second felt quite powerless. Then, in desperation, he clapped his hands and, when Neil raised his head to look at him, John found his voice.

'The petrol, you stupid bastard!'

Neil stared at him wide-eyed, still with his cigarette in the corner of his mouth but the rest of his mouth hanging open. John saw him mouth something beginning with 'f', as the realisation hit him. The two of them stood still and looked at each other, breathing and blinking. Neil was flapping his arms, unable to say a word.

Then John said, 'Step away from the bike, Neil.' Neil gaped at him.

John repeated, 'Step away from the bike.'

Neil did as he was asked, taking three steps backwards. Then he stood frozen like a tailor's dummy, his parka hanging from his shoulders, lifeless. John stepped up to him and used both hands to remove the cigarette stub from his friend's lips as gently as he could. He tossed it on the ground as if it were some horrible bug and stamped it out, then looked round at Neil.

Neil exhaled slowly, whispered, 'Thanks, mate, you saved my life.'

With that, Neil placed both hands on John's shoulders and looked him full in the face. John felt flooded with gratification that he did not step back or shrink from this contact. Instead he held Neil's stare, murmuring shakily, 'I'm glad I haven't got to ride back alone.'

They both laughed uneasily. Then John replaced the petrol cap.

After half an hour at the Wetton Pub, they were on their way again towards Ashbourne, John following in the Vespa's wake. John thought about the recent revelation, as they made their way along the A515. Over and over again he considered how he'd felt real concern for his friend's safety. This was a side of himself that he didn't know, an aspect he would not have believed actually existed. He had acted without forethought and had felt a reaction in real time, not in retrospect. He had been a participant rather than a spectator and he had taken control. Perhaps that was what was wrong with him, he never took control, he was so busy inside his own head that he allowed others to move in where he should be. It wasn't that life had no place for him, it was rather that he constantly failed to take up his place. Some other dog always beat him to pick up the stick, while he stood aside and wondered who could possibly want to throw a stick for him.

Every now and then Neil turned in his seat to look back and John knew he did it to reassure himself that his friend was still there. John also knew without any doubt that their friendship was a real thing, based on the sort of understanding of which he had previously been unaware.

Outside Neil's house in Chasetown, Neil left his scooter on the pavement and switched the engine off. John sat astride his BSA with the engine thumping quietly. He looked at Neil, slightly abashed, 'So I didn't need any petrol after all.'

Neil smiled. 'Shall we do something next weekend?'

'Sure, that would be good.'

And he meant it. This was a friendship he could cope with and feel belonged to him. He realised he looked forward to seeing Neil next time and that their friendship was somehow on a different, more equal footing. He couldn't think of anything to say but realised it didn't matter. The things he'd learned that day were understood rather than spoken. John knew Neil wouldn't mention what had happened. And why should he?

Have you ever had an electric shock through your mouth? It really is as painful and unpleasant as it sounds. Freddie Farr found out the hard way.

Freddie 'Fretboard' Farr, or Fret, as he preferred to be known, was the vocalist, lead guitarist and harmonica player for the Vultures. This multi-talented young man of just nineteen years was not only a superstar and a magnet for scantily clad groupies, but also a ham-fisted apprentice electrician with Danny Gould Electricals. Fret's boss, the long-suffering Danny, saw this musical colossus as something of a liability. Because of Fret's musical performances two or three nights a week, which he kept telling Danny were called 'gigs', Fret was constantly tired at work and his morning time-keeping was atrocious. Fret told Danny every morning that he would soon be leaving to take up a musical career and would no longer need to demean himself further with Danny Gould Electricals.

'It's a good steady job, Freddie, I lost all my bloody hair building this business up. I'll give you Top of the bloody Pops!'

'You must appreciate, Danny, that as a man of almost fifty, you cannot possibly understand the path of stardom I must tread. And it's Fret, not Freddie.'

'What is it you call yourselves, the bleeding Vultures? I'd like to vulture the lot of you, long-haired bunch of lazy gits!'

Fret raised his hands in despair, dumped his toolbox heavily into the back of the van, an ex-GPO Bedford, and slumped into the passenger seat, leaving Danny to close the rear doors. Danny rolled his eyes and passed a hand over his shiny bald pate. The two of them would then chug away in a cloud of smoke to the first call of the day – it might be rewiring a house, it might be putting in a new power point or it might be fixing a ceiling light.

The Vultures called themselves a rhythm and blues band. What that tended to mean in 1968 was that the group played a lot of blues songs plus as many Rolling Stones and Cream numbers as they were technically capable of playing. They also deigned to play a few pop songs when their young punters were getting restless and bored with 12-bar blues. The reason for that was that you cannot snog or clinch to a 12-bar without running the risk of looking really silly. On the other hand, you could look really cool doing your own special moves in a clearing on the dance floor. Youths who did this assumed that other dancers were standing back in admiration, whereas in fact they were trying to avoid the flailing hands of the isolated lunatic, who appeared to be having some sort of fit.

The Vultures had even composed some of their own songs. They tended to be about men who wanted to die because their girl had gone with another man. Only the guitar chords varied. Fret considered it very 'with it' for a young man to contemplate suicide: it made him dark and mysterious. Real blues songs were always going on about it, together with freight trains and shotguns.

Fret was the vocalist and drew great comfort from the fact that Jimi Hendrix talked his way through songs rather than singing them. Fret felt that this was his licence to be a hip vocalist while having a crap singing voice. His gyrations on stage more than made up for his vocal limitations. He was convinced that, with his long greasy dark hair, curling over his shoulders, he looked just like Jimmy Page.

As a result of Fret's remarkable versatility, he was able to play his guitar, sing the songs and, for some numbers, play harmonica too. How, you may ask, could even a virtuoso such as Fret play guitar and harmonica at once? Well, there is a little metal frame device that slips over the head of the performer and the harmonica is slotted into it. Two adjustable wing nuts at either side allow the harmonica to be hinged backwards until it lies against the performer's lips. There are, however, certain shortcomings in this device. First, as the vocalist gyrates his body, the metal device often rotates around his head, so that the harmonica is round the back of his neck. Second, should the vocalist need to look down at his score or music or whatever, he runs the risk of skinning his nostrils or even poking his eye out with his harmonica. But third, and worst of all, as Fret discovered while playing at the Fox and Goose pub, was that the harmonica holder could turn into a lethal device which dealt potential death to the highly gifted performer.

The problem is that you have to push the harmonica and its holder against the microphone. If the microphone stand should become live, so does your harmonica. The Vultures, like many groups in 1968, had deadly wiring arrangements. Wires were often pushed into main sockets and rammed in place with matchsticks. Electric shocks and even electrical fires were not unknown and on this particular evening Fret received what was known in the business as a 'belt'.

The Fox and Goose was not a rough pub. It stood beside a main road in a reasonably middle-class suburb of north Birmingham. The function room was spacious, with a generous dance floor of polished parquet, surrounded by tasteless, green patterned carpet, the sort that takes ash and vomit without complaint. At the far end was the platform upon which the group was to perform, comprising a plateau of pallets about three feet above floor level.

Dave, the keyboard player, said, 'If you ask me, that bloody platform isn't bloody safe.'

Fret replied, drawing hard on his Embassy, 'But no one is asking you, Dave, and I don't suppose Eric Clapton does a survey of his stage before he walks on to it.'

Phil, the skinny bass guitarist, chipped in, 'He probably doesn't have to. Talking of Eric Clapton, are we opening with "From Four until Late"?'

'Yep, why else would I have this ridiculous device round my neck?' Fret used both hands to point to his head.

The function room was filling up. People began to take their seats all around the dance floor and against the walls. Mingled smells of cigarettes, perfume and beer filled the stuffy air. There was an atmosphere of mounting expectation. Some of the more adventurous children came to stand by the front of the stage, gazing up at the jumble of wires, guitar cases and half-assembled drum kit. Their ears were assailed by the loud humming noises coming from the big speaker units, topped by the long, flat amplifiers with their red lights like NASA Control Centre.

'Oi, mate, what's that thing round your neck? Is it for an injury?'

Fret turned and glared down at the boy, 'You'll have an injury in a minute!'

Fret was eager to get started, particularly because he had not failed to notice some very attractive girls standing around on the dance floor.

Phil, the skinny bassist, grinned at Fret, 'Nice rumpo, Fret. I hope we can impress them.'

'I hope we can undress them,' sniggered Fret, whose most advanced sexual experience was a French kiss with his sister's friend last New Year.

The turnout was so good that, for the boys in the Vultures, it was quite intimidating. They tried to move about among the wires as deftly as they could, because to trip up would be very damaging for their image as rock legends.

Their 'roadie', Graham, did the best he could to look competent and cool. Graham sported some facial stubble which he felt gave him a certain edge with the ladies. It had taken for ever to grow and there were bare patches, but Graham was convinced that he cut an Easy Rider kind of figure.

Then there was Mick, the drummer. Mick was a broad, beefy lad with a mop of blond hair and shoulders like haystacks. Watching Mick play his drums was more like witnessing an assault than enjoying a musical experience. He seemed to bear a grudge against his semi-circular array of skins. Mick would swivel on his stool as he laid into his kit from one end to the other, the sweat dripping from the end of his nose and the muscles in his arms billowing like mainsails. Mick was not really interested in girls; his hero was Ginger Baker of Cream and Mick would have grown a beard like Ginger, had he been able.

Once all the equipment was set up, the lights were dimmed except for the spotlights trained on the stage, and something like silence settled inside the big room. Each member of the group had the 'order of service' about his person and glanced at it quickly, while Fret said a few opening words to the audience. Phil, the skinny bassist, had a most irritating habit at this point. He always insisted on last-minute reassurance and would step over to Fret and whisper in his ear, '"From Four until Late", yeh?'

'Yes, you know that. Don't ask me now,' Fret would hiss through gritted teeth and jerk his head to motion Phil back to his position.

But Phil's parting shot would be, 'It's in C, right?'

'Piss off, Phil,' Fret would whisper to Phil like a ventriloquist, while beaming at the audience.

The Vultures would then launch into the song, Fret playing both guitar and harmonica and performing the lead vocals.

Dave, on keyboard, provided backing vocals and harmony and normally got through the first song before knocking his microphone to one side with his head, so that he could no longer reach it. Dave's microphone was on a pivoting stand and once it swung away, it required a feat of gymnastics and a very long arm to pull it back. Dave was not a gymnast and his arms were not very long, so that at times the backing vocals were suddenly cut off while Dave lurched about on his stool as if trying to catch a fly.

'From Four until Late' went down well enough and was followed by 'Red House', a traditional 12-bar blues, best known as a Jimi Hendrix number. Fret's guitar solo was very well received, although he hid his delight behind a façade of nonchalance, as befitted his star status.

In fact, the whole gig went well – apart from 'the belt'. This disaster occurred as the Vultures threw themselves into one of their own numbers. Entitled 'I wanna die', it featured Fret in all three of his roles: vocalist, guitarist and harmonica player. About thirty seconds into the performance, Fret suddenly jerked backwards and through the PA system came a muffled 'Fuck!' The rock superstar was observed by his admirers shaking his head and massaging his mouth as if someone had punched him. More swear words followed and the song came to a halt.

Fret made as if to deliver an announcement to the bewildered audience gathered in the darkness but he had lost most of his power of speech, as if following an unpleasant dental appointment. Fret quickly realised he could not speak properly and gestured ferociously to skinny Phil to explain what had happened. Skinny Phil could clearly be heard whispering and pointing, 'I'm not touching that bloody microphone! Why should we both kick the bucket?'

Roadie Graham did some frantic twiddling at the mains socket, all of which looked quite lethal, and then announced with a thumbs-up that all was well. Fret found that most of the feeling had returned to his lips, although 'slow' sounded like 'shla' and 'freight train' sounded like 'hay tray'. He was wary now of imminent death but in fact the rest of the evening passed without further mishap.

The Vultures' last number, 'Ferry cross the Mersey' by Gerry and the Pacemakers, was a song to snog to, as requested by the organisers. When Fret had protested on the telephone that the Vultures 'didn't do that kind of crap', he was told to take it or leave it. Obviously he took it.

Roadie Graham began dismantling the equipment at half eleven, aided half-heartedly by the shattered members of the group. Fret knew that by the time Roadie Graham had finished loading his van it would be well after midnight. The members of the group would take at least a quarter of an hour to bicker over the cash they had received for the gig. Roadie Graham would drop each member off at his home, Fret last of all. Fret would fall into bed at about half one and dream of stardom and naked groupies.

When life-changing things occur, it often starts with something insignificant. It was late one Sunday evening that Mrs Gould, Danny's wife, knocked on the door of Fret's house.

'Hello, Mrs Farr, I'm so sorry to disturb you, I don't suppose your Fred is at home, is he?'

'Hello, Mrs Gould, whatever is the matter? Come in, you look frozen to death. Where is your husband?'

'That's why I've come, Mrs Farr, I've walked all the way. Danny's been taken into hospital.' Mrs Gould broke down on the doorstep and was ushered indoors by Fret's mother, who put her arm around the poor woman's shoulders. She knew Freddie would be away on his gig till past midnight, so she would have to wait up to tell him the news.

When Fret learned of the fate of his boss, he realised he was faced with the first real dilemma of his life. Danny Gould, now just past fifty, had suffered a mild heart attack. Once discharged from hospital, he could only work part-time. As a result, either his business would fold or Fret would have to run it until a more senior man could be appointed. Fret had by now completed his apprenticeship and was used to driving Danny's van. What was the rock star to do? The Vultures were performing at bigger and bigger venues. Skinny Phil was more confident and less of a nuisance, Roadie Graham no longer used matchsticks in electrical sockets and Dave the keyboard kept his microphone firmly in place between his nose and his right ear. Beefy Mick, more muscular than ever, produced more and more noise from his long-suffering drum kit. It all looked very promising.

The following Sunday afternoon was dank and foggy. Darkness was falling early and lights were burning in a downstairs window of Common Farm. This was where drummer Mick lived. The Victorian farmhouse had a large redundant room on the ground floor which had been taken over by the Vultures and baptised the 'practice studio'. The floor was flagged, the ceiling was high and the two tall sash windows ran with condensation. To tell the truth, the room was freezing and the stinking paraffin stove standing fuming in one corner made no impression whatever on the chill all around it. None of this bothered the Vultures, however, and the five of them sat in a circle, their breath billowing in clouds of steam, their instruments spread all around behind them.

This was a crisis meeting for the boys and a sure sign of its seriousness was the plate of fancy cakes at their feet. Mick's mother was well known as a cake-maker in the local WI and enjoyed spoiling these Giants of Rock with her creations.

Without turning to look at Fret, skinny Phil muttered, 'You can't leave, Freddie, and that's that. You *are* the Vultures. Anyone can see you are a real Vulture.'

Fret considered this for a moment and assumed it to be a compliment. He turned to skinny Phil, who added, 'I don't mean to say you have a hooked beak or anything or claws and eat dead stuff, you know what I mean.'

'Yes, thanks Phil. And it's Fret, not Freddie.'

Skinny Phil looked away and leaned forward to pick a cake with pink icing.

The real businessman among them was Roadie Graham, who always insisted on going straight to the practical details. He drove a van, he knew about things. Unlike the others, he wasn't a dreamer and he was good with money. The others went quiet when Roadie Graham spoke up, 'So Fret, you can't do any more late nights, you won't have time in the week to learn new stuff or to rehearse and your Sundays will be filled with Danny Gould's bookkeeping and accounts.'

'That's about the shape of it, yes. Otherwise I've got to tell Danny I'm leaving him and that the Vultures are going full-time professional.'

The others all agreed, that was exactly what he should do. Dave the keyboard, who rarely spoke, and had a black eye from his recent 'microphone strike', piped up, 'We are nearly there, Fret. We've got some good gigs lined up and we'll be making good money.'

Fret knew this was true and he also knew what he had to do.

It was forty years later and a crisp, sunny autumn day when the dark blue Bentley slid silently into its dedicated private parking space. The driver's door opened and out stepped a tall, distinguished-looking man with thinning grey hair swept back. It curled over his white shirt collar but was well cut and gave an impression of chic. The light grey suit was clearly made to measure, and the brogues were hand made. He was clean-shaven and his face, though lined, bore an expression of purpose and determination.

He strode towards the lift which would take him up to ground level and then to the top of the building. He stepped out onto thick carpet and glanced at his Tag Heuer. His office door was ajar and he walked in, to be joined by his secretary, who followed him all the way to his desk, reading out his messages from a notepad and ticking them as she reeled them off.

The man looked at her and smiled, pausing before sitting down. 'I'll tell you something that might make you laugh, Sheila.'

She looked up at him quizzically, 'Go on then, Mr Farr, because we've got a busy day ahead of us.'

Freddie sat down heavily in his big swivel chair. He was still grinning. He said to his secretary, 'When I've finished here this evening, I'm going to buy myself a guitar.' He looked at her as she hovered by his desk, waiting for her to laugh. He said, 'Well, don't you think that's funny, a man of sixty investing in a guitar?'

Sheila smiled and began to present him with a sheaf of papers. 'Not at all. All the big rock stars are at least your age or even older.'

'Thank you, Sheila, I assume that's some sort of compliment.'

'Well I think it is, Mr Farr. In any case, you don't need to be a rock star. Farr Electricals is one of the biggest of its kind now.'

'Well, we've installed all the electrics in an airport, a shopping centre and a theatre this year. The Les Paul will be my present to myself for a successful year.' He gazed at the papers, placed his hands on the desk top but showed no sign of starting work.

Sheila frowned, 'What is a Les Paul when it's out?'

He rolled his eyes at her in despair. 'It's a famous make of guitar, Sheila. Don't you know anything?'

'I know your tea won't appear on this desk until those papers are checked and signed.'

The man scribbled on a piece of paper which he held up to Sheila. On it she read the words: GO AWAY SHEILA AND GET MY TEA.

'Yes, Mr Farr.'

'I keep telling you Freddie will do,' but he was talking to her back as she swept away.

Five o'clock arrived and the street lights blinked on outside the Farr Building. Down on the pavement the mist was gathering and there was a smell of dead leaves. Car headlights were coming on and people in dark overcoats hurried along with their heads down.

Freddie Farr rarely left his office before seven, but this evening was different because this was the evening on which he was to buy his guitar. Although Freddie was now a man who had just about everything, the prospect of buying a guitar after so many years thrilled him. He almost ran to his car and all but walked into the door in his haste to get inside. As the Bentley swished away, up the steep ramp and onto the street, he seemed the picture of success to the passers-by on the pavement, whom he narrowly missed in his enthusiasm to get going. Freddie ignored the strange rattle he could hear, because he was certain Bentleys don't rattle. Had he known that the cause was the belt and buckle of his raincoat, which he had shut in the door, he would have been more concerned about his paintwork.

Freddie pulled up outside the music shop. He had to park askew on the pavement to prevent the Bentley from sticking out into the road. This manoeuvre did not please the pedestrians, who had to step around the car and into the road to get past.

Freddie heard himself being called a 'sodding plutocrat' and smiled in spite of himself. That really was a compliment!

He thought to himself, I wonder how long I can stay parked here before I get booked. In any case, I can hardly wander through the streets with a Les Paul. I might get mugged! The idea was to stick it straight in the vast boot of the Bentley and make off quickly.

The shop was dim inside, because they were preparing to close, but were clearly waiting for the man who had several thousand pounds to spend on a guitar. Sheila had arranged this by telephone and had told Freddie that the man on the other end of the line had sounded very odd.

'What do you mean by odd?' Freddie had asked.

'I just mean odd, Mr Farr.'

'For goodness' sake, Sheila, call me Freddie.' But Sheila had walked away.

Freddie strolled into the shop, trying to shake off some of his sixty years and to look a bit cool, in spite of the fact that part of the belt of his raincoat was soaking wet and flapping at his side. He spotted the Les Paul, posing ostentatiously on its stand with a 'reserved' notice slipped underneath the strings. A young salesman came out of the far office and weaved his way between the musical instruments towards where Freddie stood, beaming with anticipation. They were alone in the shop apart from a shadowy figure in the background who was stooping to put one of the guitars into its case, and obviously having trouble with his knees as he did so.

Freddie extended his hand to the young salesperson and was astonished when the young man thrust his own hands into his trouser pockets and mumbled uncomfortably, 'Sorry, sir, but the boss says your kind are not welcome here.'

Freddie frowned and his jaw fell in shock.

The young man, looking down at his shoes, said, 'Very sorry, sir, he says you are to – bugger off!' The poor chap was crimson in the face.

Freddie, however, was outraged and breathed in deeply, before hissing at the unfortunate salesman, 'How dare you, and how dare your boss! Where the hell is he? I want to see him right now.'

The salesman pointed shakily towards the stooping figure at the back of the shop, who rose unsteadily and came towards the two men. Freddie opened his mouth to tell him what he thought of him and to remind him just how many thousands of pounds' worth of business he had just kissed goodbye. But he was forestalled by the boss, who approached him from the shadows and who, to Freddie's irritation, was splitting his sides with laughter. The man flicked on a switch to his right and several powerful spotlights came on in the ceiling, lighting up the interior and highlighting the glossy finish of the guitars all around them.

'That got you, didn't it, Freddie? Or should I say Fret?'

Freddie was caught off balance and stared hard at the man in front of him. Of about the same vintage as himself, he had thinning grey hair and a tall, bony frame. Fret knew there was something very familiar about this person, something from long ago, another time and another era.

Then the tall thin man said, 'This number's in C, isn't it, Fret?'

Freddie's face erupted into a broad smile and he clapped the man on both shoulders, saying, 'Don't ask me now, you silly sod!'

The salesman gaped at the two men, first at one and then at the other, his mouth open, like an ornamental frog in a garden pond. Were they both mad? He thought that perhaps this was an age thing, something he could not yet comprehend.

'You old bastard, you set me up! You knew damn well I was coming this evening, because my secretary left my name. Skinny Phil! Skinny bloody Phil!'

The armchair in Phil's office was so comfortable that Freddie struggled hard to keep his eyes open. The business concluded and a nip of whisky downed, the two men looked at each other fondly. Phil talked about his joints, no longer the sort that you lit but the sort that creaked and ached; Freddie complained about his back and his failing eyesight.

'So what became of the Vultures, Phil?'

'After you left we took on a bloke called Reid, who was pathetic and unreliable. The Vultures died about six months later.'

'And now here you are, Phil, with your own store, still in the music business. Well done.'

'As for you, you bloody tycoon, I've been reading about you for a good many years and I couldn't believe my luck when I realised you were coming here. It had to be you, the right name and the right taste in guitars.'

'But you know, Phil, when I left the band I really believed it might be the wrong decision. But I couldn't desert my boss, Danny. And of course, as you know, I stayed in electrics.'

'That was a hard choice for a nineteen-year-old, Freddie.'

'Yes, Danny Gould died a couple of years later and I took over his business. That little business was the platform for everything I achieved in the years that followed.'

'You did the best for yourself by doing the best for someone else.'

Freddie toyed with the damp end of the belt of his raincoat and nodded.

At fifteen, David knew absolutely everything there was to know about absolutely everything. His self-assured swagger proved he was the master of his own domain. He knew all the words to 'Bachelor Boy', his hair shone with Tru Gel and he'd twice managed to get into the Imperial cinema to see *Dracula*. He'd even been out with Eileen Maplin, although she showed no inclination to repeat the experience. David knew she'd have a job to do better than him. Still, she was quite immature, he supposed. He could cycle with no hands in and out of the concrete bollards in front of Belcher's paper shop, until eventually he was told to bugger off. He had a tan suede jacket, jeans and winkle-picker shoes; he knew when to keep quiet about being a pupil at the local grammar school; the world was his oyster.

Imagine his surprise then, when his father said to him, 'I want you to know we're going to have to move house.'

For David this news was so shocking it made him feel quite dizzy. It heralded the uprooting of his entire life. A boy like him could only function knowing he had a familiar bolt-hole, a base around which the wheel of his life rotated. Images of his home, his front and back gardens began to fly around inside his head, but worst of all was the idea of losing his room. His little box-room bedroom was the place that defined him, he had to get back to it regularly as an animal has to seek out a waterhole.

David assumed his father must have been fired from the tax office.

'No, it's nothing like that, son.'

His father pulled on his pipe and a mysterious silence followed. David felt that saying nothing and just waiting were his best options. He watched as the bluish smoke curled around the strip light in the ceiling. His father suddenly appeared to recall that he and his mother were standing there, waiting.

'No, nothing like that,' he went on, 'no, no.'

'Well then, why have we got to leave here, Dad?'

'David, don't badger your father.'

'It's okay, Lily, I think the boy deserves an explanation.'

David toyed peevishly with the up-and-over lid of the bread-bin. This was a conspiracy to disrupt his life. How could they do this to him? His mother was looking at him with an odd expression, almost of pity, as if something dreadful was about to be revealed.

'It's the garden for one thing,' his father at last announced.

'What?' scoffed David at this ridiculous excuse.

'It's simply too much for your dad, David, the lawns, the vegetables, the fruit trees, the chickens, it just goes on for ever.' David's mother shook her head to emphasise the overwhelming level of commitment required by the garden, which had never struck David as particularly big – but then he rarely helped with it, so what would he know?

'I'm coming up fifty, lad, and I could do without all the heavy work. I want to take it easier.'

His father's lazy attitude was threatening to destabilise David's familiar world. In a moment of mad desperation, without really thinking what was coming from his mouth, David blurted out, 'I'll help you, Dad, then we can stay here in Alders Lane.'

Len Cartwright's face showed first astonishment, then total disbelief. 'That'll be the day, David. Neither you nor your brother do a tap round here. I blame your mother. Too soft, too soft by far.'

Lily put her hands on her hips and huffed and puffed. Len knew David would then start his 'but Dad' routine.

'But Dad,' David began in a rather high-pitched, tortured tone of voice, that tone of voice children resort to when they're losing control of a situation, 'but Dad, what about my schooling?' Questions about education always get serious consideration from parents, David knew, and smugly assumed he'd played a trump card.

'What do you mean, schooling?' asked Len.

'My education.'

'I know what schooling means, you idiot, I just want you to make your question clearer.'

David scanned urgently around the cluttered kitchen for inspiration.

'Well, if I leave the grammar school, my education will suffer.'

'Who said anything about leaving the grammar school?' Len eyed his son with growing irritation. David was now well and truly caught off guard. What could his father mean?

'What do you mean, Dad?'

'What do you think I mean? Work it out. You go to grammar school. Show some powers of deduction. Even your brother Peter worked that out. Mind you, he's doing O levels, so he's a bloody genius!'

'Len, please, that's enough language.' Lily pursed her lips as if she'd just noticed an unpleasant smell in the kitchen.

David fixed his eyes pleadingly on his father: 'If I can stay at the grammar school, that must mean we're not moving very far.'

'Brilliant, lad, just like Sherlock Holmes!' Len's sarcastic tone of voice was wasted on David and his face lit up as if he'd just discovered the atom.

Lily went back to the sink and resumed the washing up of the breakfast things.

David's mind raced ahead: 'Where are we moving to?'

Lily and Len glanced at each other and then at David.

'We're going across to Beacon Common Road,' said Len, blowing a stream of smoke up at the ceiling.

David took in this information for a while, his mouth open, his eyes large.

'Wow, that's a main road!' he said at last.

'It is,' agreed Len, 'it has traffic going up and down it.'

'Peter's very excited,' said Lily reassuringly, just to confirm what a wonderful idea it was.

'When did you tell Pete?' There was that slightly peevish tone again.

'This morning before he went off to deliver his papers,' Len replied, with a noticeable pause, before adding, 'while you were still in bed asleep.'

'I can't help it if I can't get a paper round.'

'Maybe you simply don't try hard enough,' said Len, 'you lost that Saturday job on the fruit and veg van, because you were too slow off the mark.'

'Leave him be, Len,' Lily said without turning from the washing-up bowl.

'See, I told you, Mother, you spoil them, spoil them both. That's what you do. I told you.'

David felt an intense need to escape to his room, shut the door and try to come to terms with all this change. His bedroom door shut off the world and those four distempered walls formed a cocoon, a hidey-hole. It was like having to digest a meal before being capable of taking any more in. Within five minutes he was there.

He cast about the little space, which was partly occupied by the diagonal, sloping area that covered the stairwell below. Ridiculous, he said to himself, that such a tiny space should have such enormous importance for him. But it did. Here were his test tubes and chemistry set, because part of him was an undiscovered research scientist. Here was his atlas of the world with red biro lines across the oceans and continents, where he'd piloted his Boeing 707, like the Airfix model on his window sill. Here were his *Eagle* annuals with wonderful colour pictures of Dan Dare and of distant planets with exotic vegetation. Here was the essential David, the complete David, the David unavailable for his friends to see. As the smell of lunch floated upstairs and under his door, he felt his world was a comfortable place which neither needed, nor could tolerate, any kind of disruption.

'David.' His mother's voice from downstairs. He ignored it.

'David.' A little more annoyed now. He couldn't ignore it any more.

'Yes.' His voice was starting to break and when he struggled to raise it, it cracked into a kind of strangled yodel. He cursed it under his breath.

'Yes what?'

'Yes, Mum.'

'Will you come down and lay the table, please.'

'Yes.'

'Yes, Mum.' There she was again.

'Yes, Mum,' he called out, as the Boeing 707 executed a perfect take-off from the window sill and rose towards its cruising level in his right hand. The aircraft was heading somewhere exotic, but David was more preoccupied with the change in his route to school.

'Let me ask you something, David.' Jenny was leaning against the green corrugated iron of the bus shelter, gazing at the passing traffic. He looked at her with a growing sense of foreboding and ran his fingers through his slicked-back hair. This gesture was far too old for him but he'd seen Gene Vincent and Elvis do it. 'Do you ever think about me when I'm not around?' She looked up at him and narrowed her eyes.

David was flummoxed. The truthful answer was no, but even he realised that was the wrong answer. He also realised he must not leave too long a pause.

'Of course I do.'

'When?'

'What do you mean, "when"?'

'What do you think I mean?' She was frowning now and tossing her long brown hair about her shoulders, as if preparing for battle. She began picking at one of the badges stitched on to her denim jacket.

All these things were very bad signs, David knew. Some quick thinking was required. He knew one or two of his friends fancied Jenny and he was secretly quite surprised it had lasted so long.

'Of course I think about you,' David replied, realising his voice sounded rather like a whine.

'Well, tell me when, give me an example.'

David was not going to get off the hook without making a concerted effort.

'I think about you – in Maths.'

Jenny rounded on him: 'You think about me in Maths! What the hell for?' Now she was beginning to sound like his mother.

'Maths is boring.'

'Oh, so Maths is boring and that's why you think about me?'

How on earth was he to resolve this? He could picture the *Eagle* comic, open at the centre page on his bed, with a superb colour cutaway diagram of a battleship, all labelled and with little figures of sailors in all the various rooms. When he got back in, he could have a good look at that. Also, the front brake on his bike wasn't gripping the wheel rim properly. There were so many things needing his attention. He turned to Jenny, his face vacant. Her eyes grew wide in disbelief, as she rumbled him.

'Oh God, David, I'm talking to a brick wall!' She reached up and rapped on his forehead with her knuckles, as if knocking on the door of an empty room. 'Hello, is anyone there? Mars calling David, Mars calling David, come in please.'

He took a step towards her and placed his hands on her waist, which brought a knowing smile to her face. She took a step to the side.

'Oh no you don't, David! That won't do for an answer.'

David guessed that there was another imminent change in his life. Mind you, the Boeing 707 was off to Hawaii this evening with Captain David at the controls. However, Captain David was about to be chucked by Jenny Roper and he was puzzled at how exactly he should feel. He knew he would be upset but as soon as *The Troubleshooters* came on the telly tonight, he would probably forget about her.

Down the rutted lane sped David's Raleigh bicycle, the mileometer clicking wildly, past all the familiar places – the Rostances' semi with the big, black Riley in the drive, the left turn into Seven Acres, where the manhole cover was always sticking up, the narrow pedestrian alleyway, where he was supposed to dismount but didn't. This was all David knew, this was his world.

The most insistent thought in his mind at this moment, as he pedalled furiously across Birmingham Road, was the fact that he only had three-speed Sturmey-Archer gears. Some of his friends had the new derailleur set-up with lots of cogs and millions of gears. His gear change was on the handlebar, theirs on the crossbar, a new kind of chic, like having the two plastic water bottles clipped on to the front with the curved metal drinking tubes sticking out. He didn't have those either, not that he ever needed a drink while cycling, but need wasn't the issue in such matters.

In a few minutes he'd be turning in to the school drive, where he had to get off his bike or risk an ear-bending. For several hours now he would have to forget about the *Pan Book of Horror* and the story in it about an insect that was placed inside a man's ear and burrowed right through his brain, then crawled out of his other ear. He also had a chemical experiment in progress, using some of his father's pipe tobacco. That hadn't gone down too well with Len, who'd called him a 'wastrel', whatever that was.

'You'd stand a better chance if you asked permission, before poking your thieving little mitts into my Gold Block baccy! It doesn't come cheap, you know. Oh, of course, you don't know, do you? I forget you live in Fairyland.'

He swung his leg over the saddle and began to scoot the bike along the school drive, with one foot on the pedal.

'Get off and push it, you stupid boy!' The red face of Mr Claybourne appeared through the open passenger window of his blue Ford Anglia. He must have opened that window purely in case there was an opportunity to shout at some unfortunate pupil. Mr Claybourne struggled to lean across and wind the window up again, as he pulled away towards the staff car park. David pondered the difficulties of getting an insect into Mr Claybourne's ear.

After Maths and Science David found himself leaning against the chain-link fence of the playground, contemplating Stella Hurst, who was practising her netball shooting skills. This involved a lot of bending and stretching and, since Stella was clad in her PE kit, this was all of particular interest to David.

Such was his interest, in fact, that he failed to notice the unwelcome figure of Miles Stentiford, whose sneer was visible almost as soon as he was. Miles was an arrogant boy, who irritated both pupils and teachers alike and made David Cartwright appear almost modest and self-effacing. David tried to look away but he was too slow.

'Well, well, if it isn't Cartwright!'

'Hello, Stentiford, fancy seeing you here.' David's tone was flat, partly because he didn't like Miles Stentiford and partly because Miles Stentiford was blocking his view of Stella Hurst.

Miles thrust his hands into his blazer pockets and looked down his freckly nose at David.

'Can I help you, Miles? Do you need directions to some distant galaxy?'

Miles ignored the sarcasm, if he even noticed it: 'I hear you're moving, Cartwright.'

David noticed that Miles's tie was askew and that it had been cut level across the end. One of his brother Pete's friends had done that, because Miles had thrown a stone at him and called him a queer. Miles had failed to take account of the fact that Pete's friend was over two years older and nearly six feet tall.

'Yes, what of it?'

Stella was now looking at David. What a nuisance Miles Stentiford was! If only he would disappear and become a colourless gas or something – like oxygen, then David could set light to him, as they'd seen in the chemistry lab.

132

'I heard your brother tell someone. He said you were upset about it.' Miles studied David closely now, to observe the effect of his words.

'I think you must have misheard him, Stenti, or you have cloth ears.' Now it was David's turn to observe Miles and to consider what he would look like if his ears really were made of cloth.

'I bet you were crying, Cartwright. Were you?'

Stella was now turning to walk away with her ball, an alluring sight for David but bad news too. His opportunity had passed and the goddess was swaying away towards the main building. David blamed Miles for this.

'Stenti, have you ever considered swallowing rat poison?'

'That sort of comment means you *were* crying, just because you're going to move house.'

'At fifteen years of age I think moving house is a matter of routine,' offered David, striking the defiant pose of a Borstal boy, as he'd seen in *The Loneliness of the Long Distance Runner* at the cinema. 'I can just take it in my stride.' He started to twiddle the red swimming badge on his left lapel, a clear sign of anxiety and one which Miles did not fail to notice.

Miles began to laugh, throwing his head back and showing a lot of spots under his chin, together with a protruding Adam's apple: 'Especially if you're only moving a few hundred yards away!'

David's eyes narrowed. He'd almost had enough of Miles. 'How do you know where I'm moving to?'

'Bush telegraph, old fruit. Beacon Common Road, I believe.'

David tried to imagine what Miles's face would feel like on the end of his fist, blood pouring from his nose and one of his incisors stuck between David's knuckles. Then Mr Henson rang the bell for the end of break.

As Miles turned to go, he said to David, 'See you, blahty boy!'

'If you had a nosebag, Stentiford, you could eat shit while you're walking along.'

David was upset to find that he felt somehow violated, as if that slob Stentiford had actually set foot in his room and rifled through his things. He didn't just blame Pete for broadcasting Cartwright family gossip but he also blamed himself for his vulnerability, this odd feeling of being a victim of some kind of assault. How far did he have to go to get completely on his own and away from other people?

'Thank you for checking before you lit that fag, Pete.'

David was sitting bolt upright on the old wooden chair at his little desk in the corner of his room. Sprawling across his off-white candlewick bedspread, Pete lay back and attempted to blow smoke rings.

'I didn't think you'd mind.' He began to look around on the bedside table and on the threadbare carpet for an ashtray.

'Reach under the bed, if you're looking for an ashtray,' said David in a miffed tone of voice.

At the point where the bed was squashed up against the wall was the quietly breathing body of Dimple, the ginger cat. Because of an injury sustained in a fight some years before, Dimple had a damaged eye which did not close properly. As a result he slept with one eye open, quite an unnerving sight for the casual observer.

'You know, Dave, I think Dimple looks more and more weird every day. He's watching me now, one eye open, one eye closed.'

'He's asleep, you berk!'

David was still sitting up very straight, as if at school. He himself wasn't aware of the fact, but he always sat like that when someone was in his room.

'You're the berk, Dave, making a stink like that with your stupid experiment.'

'Do you know what it is?' asked David, watching Dimple yawn and then go back to sleep.

'Of course I know what it is, it's Dad's pipe tobacco, you strange boy.'

'Strange boy yourself. Tell me, Pete, why have you been broadcasting all the news about us moving house?'

Pete managed a perfect smoke ring and raised his fist into the middle of it: 'How do you mean, broadcasting?'

'I've had some trouble at school, people taking the mickey, saying I'm upset about a little local house move.'

Pete sat up, leaned against the wall and began to stroke Dimple. 'I thought I was allowed to tell my friends about things happening in my life. Sorry if you don't like it.'

'You've made me sound like a ninny.'

'No, you do that yourself. You've made far too much fuss about this move and you haven't even been over to see the new house being built.'

David considered this for a moment. What Pete said was quite true. He had made a lot of fuss and no, he hadn't been to see the new house. Perhaps, if he did, his mind would be more at rest. He might just get his bike out of the shed later.

David pushed his bike rather than riding it, for he was deep in thought, as his battered suede shoes plodded across the fields of Churn Hill. The Sunday wind was warm and fitful, driving tattered grey clouds before it and threatening rain. It was a patchy, untidy sky but David was too young to appreciate the irony of how well it reflected the inside of his head.

On his right he passed the edge of 'the dump', a big abandoned sandpit a good hundred yards across, full of rusting gas cookers, saucepans, sofas, washing machines. He wondered whether his present way of life would soon be thrown away just like these discarded bits of other people's routines, these sad things that were once other people's comfy surroundings. Under the tall, whispering silver birches he pushed the clicking Raleigh, kicking little pebbles into the tufted grass, keeping to the narrow footpath with its craggy channels where the rain had washed along it and carried the red, sandy soil away.

Ahead, through the trees, he saw the daylight at the end of the track and heard the noise of traffic on Beacon Common Road.

He got on his bike and freewheeled down the last bit of pathway onto the pavement. Up the road to his left stood the green bus shelter where Jenny Roper had chucked him. Opposite him eight semi-detached houses were being built. Counting from the crown of the hill on his left, the Cartwrights' new house was to be the right-hand half of the third house down. It was called Plot 13 at the moment. David wheeled his bike across the road and stood looking at it. Plot 13 looked back at David. David was devoid of feelings. This was just a half-built house, joined to its neighbour, not standing alone like the present house in Alders Lane. He turned to glance behind him across the road, at the house that stood on slightly higher ground opposite. Again, what could he say? They were just houses. But in front of him was his new home, unglazed window frames in pink undercoat, a front garden without any boundaries looking like a scene from the Western Front, with scattered rubble and empty cement bags and paint tins.

Would he be like Dimple and keep straying back to his old home? Twice Dimple had tried that when they'd taken him on holiday with them to Prestatyn. Was David made of sterner stuff?

His mother had said to him only that morning, as he was struggling to pull his shoes on, 'For pity's sake, David, it's only five minutes' walk away, not the other end of the country.' For David it wasn't a question of distance, it was the very fact of a shift of base, of everything starting from another point.

He sat astride his bike and tried to look casual, ignoring what the wind was doing to his pop star quiff. In reality he was trying to identify 'his window', the window of the new box bedroom. Pete would have the bigger bedroom again. David didn't want it anyway. From his narrow room he could fly anywhere on the globe, he could try new chemical experiments, he could disappear inside his own imagination.

'Hello, you're the younger one of the Cartwrights, aren't you?'

David swung round to see that he was no longer alone. He knew this girl by sight but didn't know her name.

'Dave Cartwright,' he said.

She smiled. Very nice, thought David, this evening's 707 flight to Mauritius now forgotten.

'I've seen you at school,' she said, 'you're in my year. My name's Tania. I live just over there.' She pointed to a big white detached house almost opposite Plot 13. As she raised her arm to point, the flimsy cotton sleeve of her T-shirt slid back to reveal her armpit. David found this quite interesting.

'I recognise you,' he smiled back, 'we've passed in the corridor.'

'Really? I'm surprised about that. You always look as if you're in a world of your own.' It wasn't said in a hostile tone but almost as if she was intrigued by him. She smoothed down the front of her T-shirt. David found that quite interesting too.

'I suppose I am a lot of the time.' He couldn't believe he'd admitted it. He'd never done that before.

'So you'll be living opposite. That's nice.'

Yes, thought David, that *was* nice. They both stood looking towards Plot 13, the warm wind blowing around them, lifting Tania's long, brown hair, then laying it back around her shoulders. Unusually for him, David stopped fussing about his own hair and just abandoned it to the wind. He was aware instinctively that Tania was unconcerned with his quiff but was plumbing greater depths. She wanted to know who this boy was.

'Do you walk to school?' David enquired.

'Yes. You go on that, I guess?' Tania pointed to the Raleigh.

'I go on my bike from Alders Lane, where I live now.' There was a pause, after which David added cautiously, 'Er, I could walk from here, if you like.'

'If *I* like!' she laughed but again it was a pleasant laugh, without mockery.

'Well, I mean, we could walk – together.'

Now he felt a complete idiot. To his surprise she said, 'Okay.'

There was some traffic but not much. They both ignored it, facing each other but with their eyes cast down, their hands busy fiddling with their clothes and their faces.

'You're not moving very far, are you?' Here it was again, this issue about distance.

'No, just a five- or ten-minute walk.'

'Why are you leaving Alders Lane?'

'It's too much for my dad, the garden and all.'

She nodded. He was conscious that this new house was a lot smaller than Tania's opposite, so he added, 'The house in Alders Lane is much bigger than this one.' He jerked his head towards the new house.

Tania shifted her footing and reached out to put a hand on his handlebar, an almost erotically intimate gesture, or so it seemed to David. They were practically like an item just for that moment. To David, however, Tania appeared quite aloof, almost like an adult, the way she moved, the slightly low tone of her voice, not girlish at all.

'It just means more to clean,' she said.

'What?'

'A bigger house – more to clean.'

'Oh, yes, I suppose it does.'

He wondered idly what she'd do if he put his hand over hers on the handlebar but was very far from trying it. He felt almost dizzy. Tania was such a very sensible girl, she'd be able to make sense of just about anything, no mysteries for her, no panicking about little changes in a routine. He gave her a thumbs-up sign to show he understood what she was talking about. It looked laughably awkward and childish.

'Swinging,' she said, with a touch of sarcasm now.

'Swinging?' David was definitely not 'with it'.

'Swinging. That's what that bloke says on the London Palladium show on the goggle box – swinging, dodgy or Ena Sharples.'

David looked at her blankly. She was laughing at him now. 'Oh, don't fret about it, it's just a saying.'

138

Under the grey overcast sky lay the little box bedroom at Alders Lane, waiting. The test tubes stood up in the wooden rack, stained and drying. The Boeing 707 sat on the sill, waiting for a flight plan to somewhere far away. Snoozing on the candlewick bedspread, one eye open, Dimple twitched and dreamed of mice. Through the open window came the whine of the new milk float, the chinking of bottles, the jolting of tyres over the uneven lane. No more steaming heaps left by the milkman's horse with its lazy clip-clop, its leather blinkers and green foam round its mouth as it chomped absently, tramping its route. No more Mrs Brookhouse from across the lane, trotting, bent over with a bucket and shovel in hand, worrying about her vegetables and her husband's gambling. Still the box room dreamed its dream, as the world turned and everything began to change. The round electric fire, cold and copper-coloured, was collecting dust which would burn off the next time it was switched on, with that comforting acrid smell. The room told of David, the dressing gown hanging on the door, the striped pyjamas neatly folded on the pillow, the old slippers with worn-out soles placed side by side. Here was the little space that he could control in an uncertain universe, it was predictable and its laws were David's laws. But David was missing, as the day grew old and the light began to fail.

The kitchen at Alders Lane was close and steamy, filled with what used to be called a 'fug'. Pete Cartwright was making a desultory attempt to lay the table. Mr Cartwright was doing some washing up at the sink while smoking his pipe and looking out at his runner beans. Mrs Cartwright was halfway downstairs with an armful of dirty washing for tomorrow.

David's entry through the back door brought everyone to a halt, as reproachful eyes were turned upon him. Mrs Cartwright came into the kitchen, her face invisible behind the pile of dirty linen, her voice muffled, 'David, where on earth have you been? You treat this house like some sort of hotel. Your Sunday dinner is keeping warm in the oven but we're having our tea now.'

Pete held a plate to the top of his head and closed his eyes to a squint in an imitation of a Chinaman, 'Number one son come home at last velly late. Charlie Chan suspect he with rumpo.'

Pete was not surprised when his father turned from the sink, removed his pipe from his mouth and used it as a pointer. 'Peter, I won't tell you again about using that word. I don't like it and I don't want to hear it in this house.'

Foolishly Pete replied, 'Sorry, Dad, I didn't realise you don't like the word Charlie.'

'It doesn't suit you, Pete, that kind of witty comment and you know what I mean.'

David, however, seemed to be basking in some sort of personal glow, as if he had just stepped out of a warm bath. He beamed at everyone, 'Sorry I'm late Mum, Dad, Pete and I'm glad you ate without me.'

Mr Cartwright looked at his son and puffed thoughtfully. 'You're not ill, son, are you? When you're polite it always makes me think you're coming down with something.'

David looked round at his parents and his brother, bursting to impart his item of news which he was sure would impress and enthral them. 'Actually...' here he paused for dramatic effect, 'I've been over to the new house.' This announcement didn't have quite the impact he had hoped.

'Surprise, surprise! I thought you wanted to pretend it wasn't going to happen. So you went over to Beacon Common Road on that jalopy of yours.'

Pete's insult to David's bicycle had no effect whatsoever. David was still beaming, which was beginning to infuriate Pete.

'Well, what did you think of your new home?' asked his father. 'Did you spot the room that's going to be yours?'

'I didn't take much notice, to be honest. I'm looking forward to moving anyway.'

Again everyone stared at David.

Mrs Cartwright let her washing fall in a heap on the floor and looked up at her son, 'Goodness me, there has been a change in you, David! What brought this about?'

David decided not to be specific. After all, he didn't have to tell the family everything. Some things were his business. 'I suppose I just had a change of heart.'

'More like a change of tart.'

Pete looked around for appreciation of this exceptional wit but was quite taken by surprise when Len Cartwright rounded on him. 'Peter, just remember this, you may be sixteen but you're not too big for me to box your ears.'

Pete looked down and examined the back of his hands.

Lily Cartwright looked at her younger son. 'I'm glad you feel happier about moving house, regardless of what happened to change your mind.'

David thought this was a good moment to say, 'I'll have to leave the house earlier tomorrow. I thought I'd walk up to the new house and then try the walk to school from there.'

Even in those days I knew that a broom doesn't really look like a guitar. But I tucked the bristle part under my right armpit and made elaborate finger movements with my left hand up and down the scale. With my right hand I made a feeble attempt at strumming, accompanied by closed eyes and some head movements which I hoped would make me look 'sent'.

You may laugh and think that nobody, not even a boy in his early teens, could fool himself that anyone would believe they were looking at a guitarist. But, seen through a French window, by a neighbour looking over the privet hedge, it might just work. Anyway, I thought it might.

The music was 'Are you sure?' by the Allisons and 'Rubber Ball' by Bobby Vee. I got quite hot with the excitement and the fancy footwork but never allowed for an imaginary cable that would have wrapped itself around my scrawny ankles and brought me to the floor.

I wasn't sure about the difference between guitar and bass and mimed both. I could pick out both sounds and in any case, what did the details matter? If anyone had come into the dining room at that moment, I would have been mortified, with that self-consciousness that only young teens can feel. You can't laugh at yourself at that age. Your self-image is a very serious matter.

So who could be the object of this charade? Some gorgeous girl maybe, a 'teenage queen' with ponytail and stiffened petticoat? A 'Venus in blue jeans' with her clinging jumper and beehive hair? In fact it was neither of these. The person I was desperate to impress was my Uncle Joe.

Joe and Cath Hawley had been my parents' neighbours since both couples had bought their houses in 1935. Cath was a big woman with short permed hair and a dreadful smoker's cough. Even standing at her kitchen sink doing the washing up, Auntie

Cath would have a fag in the corner of her mouth and I would place bets with myself about when and where the long ash would fall. She was a housewife, though I had been told she used to be a part-time receptionist at the doctor's surgery. That seemed to me quite a posh job with considerable status, for a woman anyway. Very few women worked in those days.

Uncle Joe, in contrast, was tall and slim. He seemed immensely tall to me, though I doubt he was much over six feet. When he smoked, he would inhale deeply with a hiss and look hard at me as if unearthing all my guilty secrets. Even in those days I had guilty secrets – I smoked on building sites with my friend Patrick and I thought about Sally French, the Head Girl, and pictured her in a variety of nude poses. I genuinely believed that no other male on earth thought that way, only me.

Uncle Joe was a builder by trade but what singled him out from the other men in our lane was the fact that he was a Special Constable. He actually wore a real policeman's uniform when he marched in church parades and occasionally when he walked round the village, his hands clasped behind his back, his chin jutting forward in a masterly way with his helmet strap just below his lower lip. If I was with Patrick and we ran into Uncle Joe in uniform, I would turn crimson with pride when he bounced on his heels and looked down at me, chuckling, 'Now then, young man, what mischief have you been up to?'

'Nothing, Uncle,' I would pipe nervously, wishing my voice was a bit deeper, and looking at Patrick to make sure that he realised that this man and I knew each other.

Uncle Joe Hawley also wore a cravat at his open neck, something I had only seen on the television by the likes of my dashing heroes, Tony Britton, Raymond Francis and Adam Adamant. A cravat was the sign of a racy lifestyle and a fashionable sense of dress. My dad would never have worn a cravat.

Uncle Joe was helping to build a Mormon church in a nearby town, which only added to his status in my mind. The fact that he had no car and probably couldn't drive anyway was of little importance in those days. He had a bicycle and wore cycle clips and this in no way detracted from his stature. Patrick's dad had a car, because he worked in Birmingham. It was a Morris 'shooting brake' but this conferred no particular kudos upon him.

Uncle Joe and Auntie Cath Hawley had always been there next door, as long as I'd been around, and I assumed they always would be, because you do when you're young. Certain things never change. Your parents will always be alive and you will never leave school. I didn't believe I would ever have to start shaving and I would always be part of the 'younger generation'.

Auntie Cath and my mum both went to Jenny's Hairdresser's on Churn Hill. They would set out with greying hair and return with 'Autumn Chestnut'. They would then go to Auntie Cath's next door and drink Cherry Heering or Babycham.

When Uncle Joe came home, in his brown or white overall, Auntie Cath would say to him, 'Joe, go upstairs and wash you.' I always remember being struck by 'wash you'. Uncle Joe would look at her, as he turned to climb the stairs. There was no rebellion, no debate. Uncle Joe was a man who was somehow 'waiting'. Though often meek when chided by his wife, he was never cowed and seemed to have a private fund of consolation within him. In a similar way, he hadn't given in to baldness – no comb-over for Uncle Joe. He had his hair cut uniformly short to show a manly disdain for the ravages of time.

Then there was his smell. Uncle Joe would get off his bike after work and give off a smell of wood and cement. It was a clean smell, a very virile smell, it was a smell associated with masculine labour, lifting and working with your hands. When he asked, 'How are you, son?' and gave me a playful punch on the shoulder, it was like being accepted as a workmate, as if he didn't see me as my parents saw me. Sometimes I had an urge to punch him back and call him Joe, but of course it never happened. The age at which I could drop the title 'Uncle' seemed years away.

It was the aftershave that changed everything. We were all round at next door's – my mum and dad and my sister Lizzie. Auntie Cath laid on coffee and fish-paste sandwiches and we all sat in their lounge on the settee and the armchairs. Auntie Cath sat on a dining-room chair near the door, because she was up and down to the kitchen, and Lizzie was on the floor, leaning against mum's legs.

An evening like this was a special occasion. It was summer and the French window stood open to let in the evening air. White lilac and freshly mown grass stole into the room on the gentlest of breezes, as the light faded and the shadows slid up the wall.

But there was another smell in the room. I caught it each time Uncle Joe leaned forward in his chair to say something to my dad. It was an unusual smell, one I rarely experienced. I'd smelt it in the barber's and in earlier years I'd noticed it on the young blokes doing National Service. It was aftershave and I knew it was called Old Spice. Uncle Joe was wearing Old Spice. I wondered what Auntie Cath thought about that. In fact he was altogether different. His hair was slightly longer than usual and was combed and shiny. There was no trace of the usual grizzled stubble on his face, indeed there was a sheen on his cheeks which caught the evening light. As I stole a look at him discreetly in profile, I could see other changes too: his eyebrows had been trimmed and all the straggly bits had disappeared. The hair up his nose was cut short (I remember hoping desperately that I would never have nasal hair). Even his hairy ears had had some attention. I struggled with the idea of Auntie Cath bearing down upon him with a pair of scissors. Equally difficult to visualise was the image of this builder angling a shaving mirror towards his face, tipping it over to the magnifying side and pulling a face while snipping at his nostrils. It must have been done at the barber's. Who else could have done it?

I noticed that he refused food each time Auntie Cath heaved her huge bosom towards him, proffering sandwiches or biscuits. She didn't challenge him in her normal way and it was as if she were suddenly afraid of him. Normally she would have said, 'Eat up, Joseph, you're like a beanpole!'

And Uncle Joe would reply, 'All right, Cath, you win.'

But this evening there was no such banter and, while he looked animated and full of quick movements, she, on the other hand, was subdued, and scuttled in and out of the kitchen like a domestic.

My dad said to him, 'What are you doing with yourself these days, Joe?'

Uncle Joe sat back, winked at him and replied, 'Oh, this and that, you know.'

This surprised me, because he normally had plenty of things to say about the building trade, the local police force or St. Mary's choir, in which he was a shining light. My dad was thrown by this vague answer and covered his embarrassment by going on about his rhubarb and how good Farmer Satchwell's manure was.

Then Auntie Cath switched the light on, since it had grown quite dark, and we all blinked and looked around at each other, as if we had just discovered that there were other people around us. I looked at Uncle Joe and saw a different man, not just a working man in his early sixties, but one who smelled of the outside world, the real world, a place I knew very little about. I thought no more about this until the following Wednesday evening.

On Wednesday evenings Uncle Joe went to choir practice at St Mary's church. Auntie Cath would usually watch television or have my mum round for a game of cards.

It was about half seven when Auntie Cath walked into our kitchen red-eyed and took my mum by the hand.

'Can I talk to you a minute, May?' It was very unusual to see grown-ups in a state like this, a side they rarely showed when children were about.

I'd been busy at the kitchen sink, experimenting with soap and water on my comb to make my hair stand up firmly in a quiff. Just as I'd got it about right and was busy pouting in the little mirror, I was told, 'James, clear off and let me talk to your Auntie Cath.'

'Don't worry, mum, I'll be really quiet.'

'Yes, you will, you'll be quiet upstairs in your bedroom.' She jerked her thumb to the hall door and rolled her eyes upwards to indicate that I should go upstairs.

Obediently I left the kitchen, pushed the door softly shut and stood behind it as quietly as I could to learn something of the mysteries of the adult world. I heard the two ladies sit down at the kitchen table and I could tell that Auntie Cath was sobbing a bit.

'Oh May, I don't know how to tell you this, I'm so ashamed.'

'Whatever is it, Cath? Come on, tell me all about it.'

'Well, when Joe went off to choir as usual, I thought I'd sort out some of our old clothes for the jumble, so I went up to our bedroom. You can only have one door of our wardrobe wide open at a time. If you open both doors the whole wardrobe starts tipping forward. Why I forgot this just now, I really don't know. We've had the damn thing since long before the War. Well, I pulled both the doors open and the wardrobe started to topple towards me, so I pushed it back and closed one door.'

'Good grief, so it could have fallen on you, Cath. No wonder you were upset. I expect you got the panics.'

'I got the panics all right, May, but not about that. Some magazines slid off the top of the wardrobe. I had no idea there was anything up there apart from a hat box and some curtain material.'

'I can't see what the fuss is about. Just because a few magazines...'

'Oh May, it was what I saw in the magazines and on the covers. I can't even begin to describe it. I never knew such filth existed.'

'Oh,' said my mum in a tone of voice which told me she was suddenly in the picture. 'You mean they were – those things that men buy?' These last few words she whispered, though just loud enough for my ears to hear.

'Yes, I do mean that, May, that's exactly what I do mean. How could he? How could he?'

Then there was the sound of Auntie Cath crying again and of my mum trying to comfort her. I heard my mum's voice saying, 'After all's said and done, Cath, your Joe is just a man like any other.'

'No he's not, May!' Cath blurted loudly. 'He's my Joe!'

'Well, I suppose you'd better prepare yourself for when he gets back home. Have you thought about whether you'll discuss it with him or say nothing?'

'I expect I shall be in bed, May.'

There was a pause while my mum pondered this, then asked, 'In bed? I thought he was normally back just after nine.'

Another pause.

Then Auntie Cath replied quietly, 'Not any more, I'm afraid. Joe's taken to going for a drink after the practice. These days he comes back quite late – eleven or even later. Then he crashes about having a bath before he comes to bed. Why he needs a bath after work and again before he goes to bed, I cannot understand.'

At that point my younger sister, Lizzie, appeared from nowhere, pushed me aside and barged into the kitchen. Her irritating voice squeaked, 'Mum, Mum, James has been listening at the door. He's been listening to you and Auntie Cath.'

I was at that age when that moment would have been a suitable time for the floor to open up and swallow me whole. But I'd heard what I'd heard.

Uncle Joe had a fine tenor voice and often sang solos in church. He was known about the village for his voice and it conferred some status on him. He was our village equivalent of a minor pop star to whom people nodded in the street or jabbed each other with their elbows as they passed him, as if to say, 'That's Joe Hawley, the singer.'

Several times I had sat in church with my parents and Lizzie, watching and listening to the choir. Uncle Joe's voice soared above the others', way up to the vaulted ceiling. It was probably the only thing about him that was actually angelic. When he sang, he seemed barely human.

I cast my juvenile eye along the rest of the choir, all immaculate in their white surplices, as if divine beyond the imagination. I once heard my mum lean across and whisper in my dad's ear, indicating one of the choristers, 'There's that Alice Watts and a right piece of work she is too.'

I followed her gaze and was surprised to find that she was referring to a very attractive blonde lady who looked not unlike Kathy Kirby. What on earth could be wrong with a young woman like that? My dad nodded sagely but made no comment. I wondered what 'a piece of work' might be when it was out.

Consequently, on the next Wednesday evening, after I had had my tea and shuffled my homework round a bit on the dining-room table, I hung around Uncle Joe's front gate at Number 134. I sat on my bike with one hand resting on his wooden gatepost and closed my eyes, letting the sun play its golden light on my eyelids. I heard Uncle Joe's kitchen door open and close, followed by a clatter as he placed one foot on the pedal and pushed with the other towards the gate. As he approached, I turned the heavy iron handle and opened the gate for him.

'Well now, young James, you're at a loose end, are you? Do you want to go inside and talk to your Auntie Cath?'

I pulled the wooden gate shut behind him and weighed up what exactly I was going to say. I felt the warm evening breeze ruffling my hair. I couldn't help noticing it didn't ruffle Uncle Joe's thinning hair, because it appeared to be smeared flat with some concoction which smelt very nice but which had a visible sheen in the evening light. Even his forehead was smarmed all over with it. In addition I smelt Old Spice again, that quite exotic aroma which, for some unaccountable reason, gave me a feeling of vague unease.

I squinted up at him, 'It's really you I wanted to talk to. I don't think anyone else would understand and anyway I wouldn't want to ask them.' Uncle Joe gave me a knowing smile, as if he knew exactly what was coming.

'Got a girlfriend, have you, Jimmy?' He reached out and took my shoulder.

'No, it's not about that.' Uncle Joe's face was lit reddish gold by the dying sun and he looked like a god.

'Well, what is it about then? Spit it out. I'm on my way to church.'

I played about with the brakes on my handlebar, then looked up at him and asked, 'Uncle Joe, what does "a piece of work" mean?'

'It just means a job you've got to do, like it might be your homework.'

Suddenly embarrassed, I gave a little laugh, 'No, I mean when somebody says a person is "a right piece of work". What sort of person does that mean?'

Uncle Joe threw his head back and guffawed, so that the hair up his nose was momentarily lit up from beneath. Again he clapped me on the shoulder, 'Why, that could mean a world of things. Did you hear it said about a man or a woman?'

'My mum said it about a woman.'

Uncle Joe looked at me for several seconds as if working out just how far he could go with his answer. At length he said, 'I suppose your mum thinks this other woman likes to run around the menfolk a bit.'

I cast my mind back to the pretty blonde lady standing in the choir and nodded with new understanding. Uncle Joe, now ready to push on the pedal, asked, 'Who was your mum on about, Jimmy?'

I smiled up at him, more confident now with my new knowledge of women and the world: 'She meant that Miss Watts in your choir, the one who looks like Kathy Kirby.'

Uncle Joe's face changed for a second, as a cloud seemed to pass across it, then he grinned again, at least his mouth did but his eyes didn't.

'I should take no notice, Jimmy, it's just the sort of thing women tend to say about each other. Now I must be off, ta-ta.' With that, he clattered down the lane and I watched his tall outline move away, bathed in the blood of the late sun.

The final enlightenment came that weekend after Patrick and I had been told off by his mum for pretending her washtub was a space capsule. She had thrown an empty packet of Dreft at Patrick's head and had used a swear word. It struck me that it was one of those words I wasn't allowed to use.

I traipsed across the lane to my house, expecting to hear the commotion of plates and saucepans and the mouth-watering smell of gravy. But by the time I reached the back door to the kitchen, no such smells and no such noises had been detected. The back door was ajar and once again I heard Auntie Cath talking to my mum. This time there was no mistaking the situation. Through the gap in the doorway I beheld Auntie Cath's huge back, which bulged over the edges of the kitchen chair. I couldn't see my mum but I had the impression she was standing with her back to the stove, a position she often occupied when telling me or Lizzie our performance at school wouldn't do.

I stood just outside on the red tiles. I couldn't help thinking how much time I was spending listening to other people's conversations these days. That was the trouble with being young – your whole life was dependent upon your parents and yet they shut you out of the really important parts of their lives.

'Oh May, he's left me, Joe's left me. All he said was "Cath, I'm going now and I'm not coming back".'

'Oh my God, Cath!' said my mum. 'Couldn't you see it coming? You must have had some idea.'

'Well, he has been different for months but I never thought this would happen. We've had our ups and downs but we've been married for over thirty years, since before we moved to this house.'

'I'm so sorry, Cath. Where on earth has he gone? Has he got anywhere to go to?'

At that point Auntie Cath's voice changed and became more hostile. It was a tone of voice I'd never heard her use before: 'Yes he damn well has! He's gone off with that tart, hasn't he. He packed a bag and he's moved in with her in her little flat above the barber's in Station Road.'

I was shocked to hear Auntie Cath use the word 'tart'. My familiar world was rolling into the daylight and it wasn't a comfortable experience. I was tempted at that point to tiptoe away and try not to hear any more. If I walked down the back garden towards the compost heap at the very bottom by the chickens, I could pretend this wasn't happening and Uncle Joe would still be next door, the other side of the privet hedge, tending his runner beans. But it had happened. Grown-up life seemed to be made up of this kind of thing all the time. I'd heard about husbands and wives splitting up but until now it had never seemed a reality.

'What tart is that?' ventured my mum.

'What tart?' scoffed Auntie Cath, 'I'll tell you what tart, May. It's that little hussy Alice Watts, that's who it is. She's barely thirty if she's a day! It's disgusting, that's what it is. That's what all those awful magazines were about, he was thinking of her when he should have been thinking of me.'

This last comment I found very difficult to comprehend. The idea of Auntie Cath posing naked in a magazine was beyond my powers of imagination. She must have weighed nearly twenty stone.

'May, he's more than thirty years older than her. What can they see in each other?'

There was a pause, during which my mum was probably trying not to state the obvious. Even I had a very clear idea what Uncle Joe might see in Miss Watts. My mum knew this but didn't want to say it, nor did she want to ask what Miss Watts might see in Uncle Joe.

'Good God, May,' Auntie Cath went on, 'he's over sixty and he's got piles!'

This completely baffled me – piles of what? I assumed she meant he had a lot of money, though surely this would attract Miss Watts rather than put her off.

As the warm, sunny days rolled by, my head was filled with the sad image of Auntie Cath moping about in Number 134, sobbing now and then and wondering what had happened to her life. What made it sadder still was the fact that she was such a large lady and had a way of walking in which she lurched from side to side, as she shifted her weight from one foot to the other. Slim people didn't do that. My mum didn't walk like that. I pictured the long, grey ash on the end of her cigarette and wondered whether she let it drop on the carpet. I heard Mum telling one of her friends down at the shops that Auntie Cath had stopped bothering about the house. I thought about Uncle Joe with his cravat and his Old Spice and tried to fathom how he could have been so cruel. What could possibly make quite an old man give up his whole life and start afresh with somebody new? I simply had no experience of this sort of thing and all my previous values began to teeter, as I scrabbled for understanding. My parents told me to mind my own business and that what went on among adults behind closed doors was their concern. My dad told me I would understand when I was older and that I shouldn't worry myself about it now. He was not to know that understanding would come much more quickly than he had implied.

I was walking down Portland Road on my way to the pictures to see *The Guns of Navarone*. I was just between the Conservative Club and Mr Ecob's the dentist, with my head down looking at the pavement, my thoughts many miles away, although I was also fascinated by the changing shape of my shadow as it rippled over the tarmac. I chanced to look up to see how far I had to go and saw that I was catching up with two grown-ups ahead of me. They were walking much more slowly and I shortened my step, because I wanted to avoid gaining on them.

I don't know how long it took for me to realise that the man was Uncle Joe and the woman was Miss Watts. I was spellbound as I watched them walking along. Miss Watts was much shorter than Uncle Joe and craned her neck to look up at him. The look of adoration on her face, even though seen only in profile, struck me vividly. I'd never seen a look like that before, except in the movies. Not only were they hand in hand, but their arms were somehow entwined and they were leaning against each other as they walked. Uncle Joe stood much taller and looked to me something like a Wild West hero. Twice he turned to look down at Miss Watts and I saw a man I barely recognised.

They walked slowly on, the sunlight dancing all around them, and suddenly I understood everything. Becoming a man wasn't simply a matter of growing taller. All at once I understood why men and women do such crazy things and get into so much trouble. I stood still on the pavement and watched as the shadows of summer flickered over them and they walked step by step out of my life.

A GIFT OF LILIES

It wasn't all that usual to see a tall young man in an Afghan coat walking down Anchor Road on a Saturday morning. But there he was, with his shoulder-length brown hair and the shadow of a beard around his pale face. His bell-bottomed jeans flapped around his ankles in the mild summer wind. Aldridge wasn't used to students and Keith Golder drew some funny looks and muttered comments from the locals.

'To think we pay taxes for the likes of that thing, Marje! A good dose of National Service would have put him right. Nancy-boy beatnik.'

'Sshh, George, he'll hear you.'

'Don't bloody care if he does! I suppose he believes in free love and drugs and all that drivel.'

If Keith heard this, it certainly didn't bother him. By the end of the week he would be going back up to Liverpool University to receive his degree. He felt sure that within a few years he would be hiring and firing men like that. On he walked, past the shops on his left, towards the traffic island at Northgate and the post office where he was heading. It was strange, no one cast a second glance at him in Liverpool, where he was one among thousands of students. But here, in this parochial little town in South Staffordshire, he felt rather like an exhibit, he felt completely out of place.

He checked his reflection in the window of the estate agent and was just about to pass the florist when he stopped dead in his tracks. A memory of the past slid into his head, a memory of early days at the local grammar school.

From out of the shop strode a large, elderly man of about seventy, bearing a big bunch of flowers. He was well over six feet tall and thickset, with a bald head and a rugged clean-shaven face. Keith might have recognised him right away, had it not been for the light grey suit and the immaculate white shirt.

Keith looked down instinctively for the big hobnail boots but saw instead a pair of highly polished dark brown brogues.

'Mr Davies?' muttered Keith in astonishment.

The big man paused in mid-stride and turned. He looked the odd young man up and down, as his expression of contempt melted away and his jaw slowly fell: 'Well, rot my gut! It's Keith, isn't it?' He turned to put the wind at his back and, in so doing, almost thrust his bunch of flowers into Keith's face. Mr Davies gave a jovial laugh and prodded the Afghan coat with a large index finger: 'I'm not mistaken, am I? You are Keith from up the Barr Common?'

With the loosely wrapped flowers hovering just underneath his chin, Keith had the strange feeling he was being interviewed and should speak into this paper trumpet, as if it were a microphone.

'Mr Davies, I thought I recognised you,' said Keith, as the flowers clustered around his chin, their perfume making his eyes water. 'It must be seven or eight years since I worked on your van.'

Keith tried to step back from the flowers and the wrapping paper but his coat was somehow still caught up in them. The wind was gradually opening the paper cone, so that it appeared that Keith would soon be wearing it like a bib.

'I'm twenty-one now,' offered Keith gaily, discreetly pushing the paper away, to avoid eating it.

'And I'm bloody seventy, lad! September 14th 1898. I was a war baby just like you but in my case it was the African War.' He readjusted the wrapping around his flowers, poking Keith several times in the face.

In the pause that followed, Keith felt he should supply details of his progress, while Mr Davies continued to wrestle with his large bunch of flowers.

'I get my degree next week at Liverpool University.'

Mr Davies stepped back and appraised the strange young man. Then he laughed, 'Bloody egghead! I knew you'd never be able to get a proper job.'

As he reached out to pat Keith affectionately on the shoulder, he completely lost control of his flowers and their rebellious paper. The two totally mismatched men struggled together to control the large sheet of wrapping paper and to force it back into something resembling a cone.

Then it was Keith's turn to look Mr Davies up and down. He had never seen him dressed in anything other than his old working clothes, the worn cow gown, the greasy flat cap and the hobnail boots. This was an altogether different man.

'You look really gen in that suit.'

'Really what?'

'Really gen, it means really good.'

'Well, talk English, lad. I'm not a bleeding hippie, nor ever likely to be one at my age. I retired last year but I still go up and see Lorna once a week. You remember Lorna, lad.'

Keith racked his brains and replied, 'I don't think I remember a Lorna.'

Mr Davies pulled a face in exasperation and raised his eyes to heaven, 'Mrs Roddick, you remember Mrs Roddick.' Mr Davies opened his eyes wide and arched his eyebrows meaningfully, as if to convey some supplementary information.

Keith's mind rushed back to Old Scott Farm on the western side of Barr Beacon and to Mrs Roddick, the glamorous widow. A wind which seemed to come from years past tousled his hair. He didn't even need to close his eyes in order to see the broad, squat farm cottage, its ill-fitting door ajar and that awful Trad Jazz coming from indoors. Mr Davies had arched his eyebrows in a similar way all those years ago when he'd announced to Keith that Mrs Roddick was a widow. During Mr Davies's hour with her every Saturday lunchtime Keith recalled sweeping the van out and tidying everything up between the morning and afternoon rounds. Mr Davies had spent the hour in the company of Mrs Roddick. Keith smiled at his own naivety. How different the world looked when you were just fourteen!

He looked up at Mr Davies with a new respect and new kind of recognition.

'You had a few cups of tea with Mrs Roddick, didn't you?'

'Aye lad, I certainly did, and lashings of sugar in all of them, if you know what I mean.' He jabbed Keith with his elbow and winked at him, satisfied now that things were on a different footing. Keith felt a sense of privilege at being invited to see things from this new, adult point of view.

'I'm on my way up there now with these lilies.' He looked down at the half-open flowers, his face soft and reverent, as if he were looking down at a sleeping child. He added, as if talking to himself, 'She likes lilies, does Lorna, likes them a lot she does.'

'Well, you're certainly dressed for the part, Mr Davies.'

Still the big man's eyes had a softness about them and his lips compressed into a diffident smile: 'I'll be honest with you, Keith, I'm going to ask her to marry me. She might tell me to bugger off, I don't know, but I've got a bit put by. I'm not a poor man but I'm not a young man either.'

Keith understood the implication of all this and searched for an appropriate comment, the sort of thing a more mature man might come up with. He said, 'She seemed more than happy to invite you in every week.'

'And once a week ever since. But there's a world of difference between that – ' here he paused to check that Keith understood what 'that' was – 'and the institution of marriage.'

Keith nodded to show he completely understood the distinction.

'So I shall be taking these here lilies to Lorna and bending my knee in her back kitchen.'

'Well, I wish you luck, and maybe next time I see you, you'll be a married man.'

'Thank you, lad, maybe I will.'

In no way could Lorna Roddick be considered beautiful or even pretty from close to. Rather she was 'handsome'. That is to say, her features, though regular, were large and well-defined, rather than small or dainty. Her days spent outdoors, when the farm had been busy and her husband was alive, had given her a tawny, lightly tanned face. Her eyes were strikingly green like onyx.

Her dry, brown hair was scragged back into a tight ponytail, so tight that it forced her eyes unnaturally wide open. Her lips were still full for a woman of forty-something but there was a little too much pink lipstick on them, just as there was a little too much mascara and eye-shadow around her eyes. She was quite tall, with a trim waist and long, slim legs which she showed to advantage in her tight, faded denims. Lorna always went barefoot in the house and her movements were supple and loose-limbed. So this was no beauty, it's true, although Lorna Roddick was well able to make a man pause to look at her twice and say to himself, 'She's well put together, I'll give her that.'

Bart Davies had said it many times.

Under the low, beamed ceiling of Lorna's sitting room she was being appraised by Ruby Glover, her friend from Perry Barr. Ruby was slightly irritated by the secretive little smirk on Lorna's face and by the way she flourished her cigarette, as if being auditioned for a movie. Ruby was waiting for an answer to her question, though none seemed to be forthcoming.

'Well?' Ruby asked once again, leaning forward in her armchair.

'Well what?'

'Oh for goodness' sake, Lorna, if you don't want to talk about it, why did you bring the subject up in the first place?'

Lorna shifted in her chair and exhaled a cloud of blue smoke which hung in the light from the low window. 'I said my relationship was getting more serious, that's all, I didn't expect to get the third degree.'

Ruby Glover was older than her friend. Her mouth turned down at the corners in an expression of permanent disapproval. Even in Lorna's sitting room she wore her green felt hat with its sprinkling of artificial white chrysanthemums. She looked every inch a visitor, her over-large handbag sitting on her lap like a puppy, her sensibly shod feet together on the patterned carpet.

Ruby had been a district nurse until her retirement and had retained a no-nonsense manner with people, an assumption that everyone was trying to short-change her. Nonetheless she was a caring person and it came across in spite of her brusque exterior. Lorna knew this and valued it. Lorna was no fool.

After another long pull on her cigarette, Lorna smiled, tapped off her long ash and said, 'Look, Ruby, if I'm going to discuss this with someone, I want that someone to be you. You understand people so well...' here Lorna paused and noticed Ruby smirking with gratification at this compliment, so she added, 'although you're a grump!'

The smirk snapped off and Ruby's mouth turned even further down than usual: 'Well really, Lorna, I don't think that's a very nice...'

'I don't intend to sound rude, you know that, but I need to know what you think.'

Ruby disapproved of cigarettes and was not amused at the toxic cloud floating around her face.

'Who is this man who's taken such a hold over you? To be honest, Lorna, I never thought you'd remarry after poor Ted. You're not short of money, if you don't mind my saying so, and you've hinted that some of this land', she waved her hand vaguely towards the window, 'is going to be built on, which means you will be a rich woman. I'm well aware that men show an interest in you but I can't see that you need a pair of boots under your kitchen table.'

'It's not about money. This one is getting rather special.'

'I can tell by your face, my dear. Tell me, what was it that actually won your heart?'

Lorna thought for a long while, then replied, 'He once bought me some lilies.'

'And that did it?' asked Ruby in disbelief.

'Yes, that and other things, but especially the lilies.'

'Some people say lilies are for funerals,' Ruby offered, studying her friend closely.

'Or for weddings,' said Lorna defiantly.

'What is it about lilies?'

'They smell clean, they smell of the future,' Lorna's eyes were far away, 'and they look innocent, as if this world hasn't touched them. White for innocence.'

Ruby had no patience for poetry or philosophy. For her lilies meant only messy pollen that caused stains. She said as much to Lorna.

Lorna said, 'The stain is part of the magic. It won't wash out, it stays with you like the man himself. He won't be washed away.'

'Very well, who is the man?' demanded Ruby.

There followed a long pause, as is usually the case before a bombshell is dropped. It was as if the room itself held its breath, as golden dust danced in the sloping sunlight and there was only the heavy tick-tock of the grandmother clock to measure out the passage of time. Lorna wore that expression of a woman who has a secret which she is bursting to share with others but wants to hold the waiting moment for ever. Ruby was reaching that point at which anticipation sours into irritation, so she cocked her head and pursed her lips, ignoring another billow of cigarette smoke which was sailing her way.

Then Lorna said, 'Bart Davies.'

Ruby's expression was one of confusion and, frowning, she asked, 'Who? I don't know any Bert.'

'Not Bert, Ruby, Bart. It's short for Bartholomew.'

'Never heard of him,' said Ruby rather sharply and snapped her handbag shut, as if to hint to Lorna that this conversation was drawing to a close.

'You do know Bart Davies, Ruby – the fruit and veg man.' Lorna nodded at her vigorously, willing her to remember.

Then gradually the light began to dawn and Ruby's eyes and mouth opened together. She leaned back in her chair, as though her spine and neck had collapsed. Then, after a strange choking sound, not unlike a death rattle, she said, 'Not *old* Mr Davies, that scruffy man in that dreadful van?'

Not in the least put out, Lorna smiled and spread her hands over the arms of her chair. 'You should see him in a suit, Ruby, then you'd change your mind.'

'But good heavens, Lorna, he must be all of seventy if he's a day!'

Lorna drew her feet up onto the chair and clasped her hands around her ankles: 'You're exactly right, Ruby, he is seventy and he does look very different when he's dressed smartly, almost like a military man.'

Ruby replied tartly, 'He's after your money, that's what he's after, that and your – er...' Ruby nodded several times at Lorna, then added, 'You know what I mean.' Then she turned her nose up as if the whole idea was quite distasteful to her.

'He's been visiting me once a week for a long time now. He comes in for an hour on a Saturday while he's doing his round.'

Ruby raised her hand, 'That's more than enough, Lorna, I don't wish to know any more.'

'Oh Ruby, that's one of the reasons why I like you so much, you can be so prudish.'

'I've seen enough men's and women's bits and pieces to last me a lifetime and I suppose that's why I never married.'

Lorna looked at her and smiled for a few moments, then became more serious: 'Wish me well, Ruby, I only want you to wish me well. As for money, Bart is well provided. He's a saver, a hoarder. He's been salting money away for many years, so believe me, he doesn't need any money of mine. And his is cash, mine is land. His money can be got at, so he's the one who needs to watch out.' Lorna tipped her head back and laughed an uninhibited laugh, before drawing on her cigarette again.

Ruby managed a smile in spite of herself: 'So you've been getting more than just fruit and veg from Bert.'

'Bart, Ruby, his name is Bart, and the other stuff is my business.'

The two women looked at each other and then suddenly, without warning, they both burst out laughing.

The lane up to Old Scott Farm was steep and narrow. A dense tree canopy whispered overhead and cast racing patterns of light and shade over the potholed surface. Rumbling up the hill came Mr Davies's unwieldy van, clouds of blue smoke pumping out from somewhere underneath and the scrunching of gears advertising its upward struggle. He kept his eyes on the lane ahead, because each violent lurch threatened to derail his vehicle and send it careering onto the verge.

Nowadays there was no weight in the back, so that the whole vehicle bounced around like a big dipper ride, Mr Davies resolute at the big dish steering wheel, a stub of cigarette just visible in the corner of his mouth. All he carried in the back these days was a bit of fruit and veg for his own consumption or as a gift for Mrs Roddick. Propped up against a rear wheel arch were a half-full potato sack, a box of tomatoes and a crate of cooking apples. In former times the smell of these items would have filled the vehicle, together with the usual lethal exhaust fumes. Today, however, a new and all-pervading odour spread out from the passenger seat. It came from the lilies, lying in their wrapper next to Mr Davies. Now and then he would steal a glance at them and smile to himself with the satisfaction of a job well done.

In a few minutes he would pull up opposite Old Scott Farm, he would check his face and his suit and his shiny brogues, he would step firmly down the little sloping path and knock on the door. Lorna would open it and he would ask her to marry him. He didn't know how he would be received but he believed his chances were good. It was an unlikely union maybe, but nonetheless worthwhile for all that.

On and on he went into the flickering sunshine, visualising Lorna's smile as she opened the door to him, standing on tiptoe in her bare feet to kiss him on the cheek. The smell of the lilies spoke to him of the end of his old life and of the opening up of something new. As he breathed in their odour, he had that exhilarating feeling that anything was possible. He knew, in the way that you do as you grow older, that this was one of those snapshot moments that will always be remembered.

The next bump dislodged the goods in the back and he heard several thumps, followed by the sound of vegetables and fruit rolling about behind him. Unperturbed, he drove on, smiling into the dirty windscreen. There was no reason to pull up, he could sort it out at the farm. After all, it was only a sack of spuds.

THE AUTHOR

David Ayres was a language teacher for many years and held several Head of Languages posts at secondary schools in the West Midlands, before turning his attention to special needs education.

He began writing poetry and short stories at an early age and won an award for English literature at school when he was just seventeen. David's work has been published regularly in magazines and anthologies and writing is still his passion in life.

Although he has retired from the day job he continues writing because, as he tells people, he can't help it. His main reason for writing has always been in order to be read.

David is currently living in Lichfield in Staffordshire.

More details are available from
www.hollandparkpress.co.uk/ayres

Holland Park Press is a unique publishing initiative. It gives contemporary Dutch writers the opportunity to be published in Dutch and English. We also publish new works written in English and translations of classic Dutch novels.

To

- Find out more
- Learn more about David Ayres
- Discover other interesting books
- Read our unique Anglo-Dutch magazine
- Practice your writing skills
- Take part in discussions
- Or just make a comment

Visit

www.hollandparkpress.co.uk